BLACK
TIDE

BLACK TIDE

JOHN WINGATE

Weidenfeld and Nicolson
London

To DICKIE RICHARDSON
visionary, communicator, seaman,
– and to ANN
I dedicate this book with gratitude.

Do not look back,
And do not dream about the future either.
It will neither give you back the past nor satisfy
your other daydreams.
Your duty, your reward, your destiny, are here and now.

Dag Hammarskjöld,
First Secretary-General, United Nations.

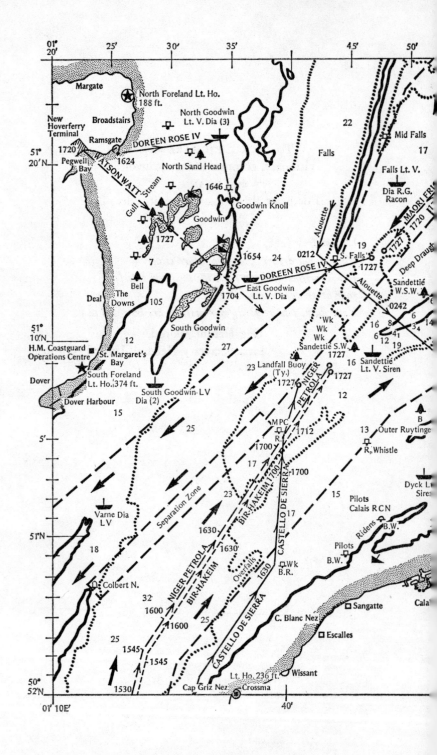

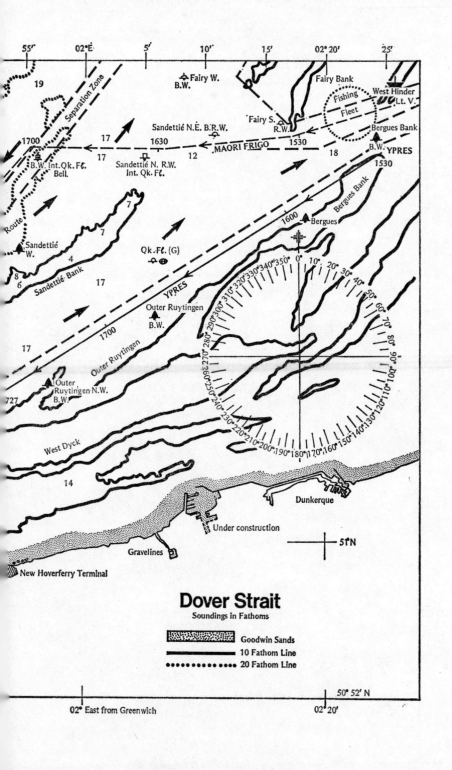

Dover Strait

Soundings in Fathoms

░░░░░	Goodwin Sands
▬▬▬	10 Fathom Line
•••••••••	20 Fathom Line

02° East from Greenwich

02° 20'

Contents

Acknowledgments

This book owes its existence to the kindness of many seafarers, those men who traditionally ask for little but give much. During my research, when to be at sea again was a delight, I met nothing but goodwill wherever I went and to whomever I talked.

The account which follows is too near reality for comfort. The manuscript has been double-checked by those professionals who have given so much of their time and patience, so that the record is correct in detail: it is only the different juxtaposition of events that renders this book fiction.

Amongst the many to whom I am so indebted, I particularly wish to thank Captain David Kilner whose hospitality I once enjoyed on board his ship. He opened the door through which I had only to pass to complete my research.

My gratitude is due to all those who helped, but especially I wish to thank the following:

The Directors of Cunard–Brocklebank and Captain A. C. Sprigings, Operations Manager, who generously gave me the opportunity of going to sea in a modern ship of their container fleet.

Captain Lionel Brown, Master of ACT 6, who made me so welcome and who put up with me during a trying voyage. I count myself privileged to have sailed with a seaman of his calibre and to have shared his friendship. I will long remember ACT 6, and especially the kindness of her officers and men, and of her relieving

Master, Captain Hunt. They showed much patience and good humour, as they revealed to me the marvels of their ship and of the container revolution.

Mr D. Wise, Director-Operations of Hoverlloyd, and his hover-craft captain and officers who provided me the opportunity of witnessing the skill and the prudence by which their unique craft are operated.

Mr W. B. Laidlaw, Passenger Manager, P & O Normandy Ferries; Captain Conway and his officers, of MV *Dragon* who showed me such courtesy.

Mr Michael Richey, MBE, Director of the Royal Institute of Navigation, whose foresight and initiative set in train the advances that have been made, and his secretary, Mr Derry Nicolson, for his practical help and guidance.

Captain Richard Emden, DSC, Royal Navy (Ret'd), Inspector, Her Majesty's Coastguard, and his Coastguard officers and Coastguards at the Dover Straits Operations Centre, St Margaret's Bay. Under his leadership, his efficient team has pioneered the Surveillance and Information Service which provides the shipping with the vital information it needs, when making the passage of the Straits of Dover. I am extremely grateful to Captain Emden for his advice and for his help.

Nineteen miles on the other side of the Channel, Monsieur Bernard, Officer-in-Charge of the CROSSMA Operations Centre at Cap Gris Nez, with the approval of Monsieur Jaffray, *Adminis-trateur-en-Chef des Affaires Maritimes,* Jobourg, allowed me a free-run of their organization and made me very welcome. They gave me the invaluable help which I sought. To Monsieur Bernard and his staff, I also offer my thanks.

Finally, it is difficult to express adequately the debt I (and, assuredly, many others) owe to Lieutenant-Commander R. B. Richardson, Royal Navy, (Ret'd), FRIN. As one-time Harbour Master of the Port of London, leader of its pioneering Navigation Service for almost two decades, and now a marine consultant of international repute, there are few men better qualified to express their views on this vital matter of shipping and its traffic control. It is no exaggeration to claim that the Thames Navigation

Service, which he and his team pioneered, has been a prime force behind world evolution in this field.

Without his vision and enthusiasm, without his aid and the time he devoted to checking my manuscript, and without his encouragement this book would never have been written.

10 October 1976   *John Wingate*

Introduction

After the *Ypres* Inquiry, about which there had been many misgivings, an independent committee of shipowners and seafaring unions asked several of us men from the shipping and legal world to find out the real truth behind the fundamental causes which led to the final catastrophe. For most people's tastes, there had been too much whitewashing, even after making allowances for much missing evidence.

As usual, it was easy to lay blame on the 'flags of convenience', and particularly upon *Niger Petrola*. But with such congestion as there is in the Straits of Dover, a disaster of this magnitude can have been a matter only of time. Fate is never impatient, biding her time until she holds all the cards. They happen every day, the little incidents. It is when they are compounded that the devil's brew simmers to produce a potential disaster of horrendous proportions.

Each of the named ships, in her own way, contributed towards 'the Downs Incident', as it euphemistically became known; but, it must be remembered, many other ships were continuing to pass normally through the Straits upon their lawful occasions at the moment when the catastrophe occurred.

Can the responsibility for this tragedy be so neatly shifted on to the shoulders of the ship operators? We take for granted (though most of us neither know nor care) the risks and the strains which our ship masters endure to carry to our shores the vital supplies which keep the wheels of industry turning. Without the regular delivery from around the world of our food and raw materials, we, an island race, would starve within three weeks.

So often in wartime was this fact hammered into us. But in our computerized and contemporary peacetime society, this truism remains unchanged. More than ever before, our industry depends upon the fine balance and timely delivery of its essential supplies. Are we not guilty of criminal complacency, if we fail to create conditions for ships which are standardized and as safe as possible?

This book is the record, the result of patient, confidential and painstaking inquiry, of 'the Downs Incident' and the subsequent horror. For most of us, and particularly for those who live along the tide-swept south coast, time has begun to heal the wounds; but we are drifting too easily into a serene euphoria, content to excuse by saying, 'It can never happen again.'

Our French friends, only nineteen miles distant, suffer the same expense and the identical horrors of pollution and catastrophe. These are our coasts, our beaches, our ports.

With them we must jointly take energetic action *now*, policing and surveilling the Straits if need be. If we fail to act in concord, it can only be a matter of time before another and perhaps even more horrific calamity strikes at us again from the sea that was once our shield – but which is now a constant, potential menace.

The statistics shown overleaf speak for themselves.

For the seventeen-year period between 1958 and 1974, the number of total losses due to collision was just under 2000: 117 a year, or one every three days.

Nearly sixty per cent of these total loss collisions occurred in the coastal waters of north-western Europe: seventy per year, or one every five days.

Of these, twenty-five per cent occurred in the southern North Sea or Dover Straits: seventeen per year or one total loss due to collision every three weeks.

Can we afford to wait?

Major tanker disasters for Lloyds.

DATE		WEIGHT (dead weight) tons	HULL VALUE ($ millions)
March 1967	*Torrey Canyon*	123,000	16·5
July 1969	*Silja*	100,506	10
October 1969	*Seven Skies*	97,550	9·6*
December 1969	*Marpessa*	207,000	16*
December 1969	*Mactra*	205,000	16*
December 1969	*King Haakon VII*	209,000	16
June 1970	*Thorland*	50,230	3·6
September 1970	*Aquarius*	214,000	23
October 1970	*Pacific Glory*	77,648	7·5
November 1970	*Thames Maru*	72,148	7.2*
December 1970	*Ragny*	17,310	1·5*
January 1971	*Texaco Caribbean*	20,545	5·2
January 1971	*Universe Patriot*	157,602	15·6
February 1971	*Ferncastle*	97,150	12·8
March 1971	*Wafra*	49,672	6·5
March 1971	*Ocean Bridge*	113,370	10·5
December 1971	*Elisabeth Knudsen*	216,187	28
December 1972	*Sea Star*	63,989	12
January 1973	*Hallanger*	20,416	5
March 1973	*Igara*	145,000*	22·5*
June 1973	*Conoco Britannia*	117,000*	21
November 1973	*Golar Patricia*	217,000*	24
December 1973	*Elwood Mead*	119,000*	25
February 1974	*Nai Giovanna*	138,850	24*
April 1975	*Cactus Queen*	158,000*	16*
April 1975	*Tosa Maru*	85,000*	6·5*
August 1975	*Globtik Sun*	54,768	10·6*
October 1975	*Kriti Sun*	123,000	30
January 1976	*Berge Istra*	223,913	18·2

* approximately

PART
ONE

CHAPTER I

ss *Bir-Hakeim,*
Lightening Tanker

Thursday, 3 June
Wind: Force 4, wsw
Visibility: 3 miles

She emerged from the hazy horizon like a spectre: a mastodon looming out of the mist. Her after bridge structure seemed disconnected from her fo'c'sle-head, she was so laden and trimmed-down in the water. In this visibility, Captain Gael Le Bihan had difficulty, even through his binoculars, in seeing the long, low freeboard of the Very Large Crude Carrier (VLCC) that had steamed the long passage from the Gulf. She was the *Niger Petrola*, 220,000 tons and she wore the Liberian flag of convenience. This dubious distinction gave little satisfaction to the Breton master of *Bir-Hakeim* who was wedged into the corner of the port wing of his own tanker, a ship of which he was discreetly proud.

Bir-Hakeim was the first of Universal International's two lightening tankers. Each of 80,000 tons, they were being used to lighten the VLCCs so that they could enter the estuaries and harbours to discharge their cargoes at the terminals. It would be a few years yet before the full quota of off-shore terminals was completed.

Le Bihan, a competent, restless and obstinate man, picked up the R/T phone which was connected in the wings:

'*Bonjour, capitaine* . . . This is *Bir-Hakeim*, Captain Le Bihan speaking. What is your course and speed, please Captain? Are you happy if I start running in now?'

Le Bihan was taking no chances with *Niger Petrola*. Even though her captain was English, she was an unknown quantity as far as Le Bihan was concerned. He, Le Bihan, was the lightening master, so was in charge of the operation, thank God. He never enjoyed taking *Bir-Hakeim* alongside an inexperienced VLCC, so that in this failing visibility he felt even less enthusiastic. The loud-speaker crackled in reply and an English voice answered.

'This is *Niger Petrola*. Captain Gratton speaking. Glad to see you, Captain. I'm all ready. As you suggested last night, my course 120°, speed four knots.' The English master seemed relaxed, friendly. 'It's all yours now. Over . . '

'*Merci* . . . My speed five-and-half. Please steady on 120°.'

Gael Le Bihan replaced the microphone and turned towards his own wheelhouse. Gaston was on the wheel which was now in 'hand'; he was an old seaman and the best helmsman in the ship. Taking an 80,000-ton tanker alongside another monster almost three times the size, in this dark and hazy visibility, both ships under way in waters that were becoming too congested, and with little sea-room or depth in which to manoeuvre, demanded much of a master's nerve. The Breton gave an inaudible grunt of satisfaction.

Le Bihan was Universal's second senior master and he was secretly pleased at having been selected as their senior lightening master. He had become restless and was becoming stale when suddenly he had been asked to develop the company's lightening operations. A month later he had found himself in command of this fine ship, so surprisingly easy to handle with her large single propeller. He had discovered a new zest and he enjoyed the exhilaration of bringing his ship, port side-to, alongside the VLCCs: huge rubber fenders, the size and shape of a midget-submarine, were slung on davits from *Bir-Hakeim*'s port side.

Surprisingly in this poor visibility, there was a stiff breeze blowing from the south-west; not enough, Le Bihan thought, to affect the steering. There was little sea running as yet, and, rather than lose time by altering away to the northward and so closing the shipping lanes, he would stick to his original plan – the lesser of two evils.

'Closed up at lightening stations, sir.'

The report came through on the internal intercom from Jean-

Paul Boury, his chief officer of the port watch. In its wisdom, the company had deliberately over-manned these two lighteners, so that the officers should not suffer fatigue: a chief officer was in charge of each watch. Unfortunately, Boury had joined only recently and was new to the lightening operation. To give him experience Le Bihan had placed Boury in charge on the main deck where the break-away party stood-by, near the port crane. Axes, leviathan spanners, strops, fire extinguishers and scaling ladders, all were ready in case of emergency. It was tricky enough taking the ship alongside, but, once the hoses were connected, it was dangerous to break-away in a hurry if an emergency threatened.

The breeze hummed over the top of the wind vanes in the bridge wing where Le Bihan stood, a solitary figure. He could hear the distant clatter of the wires across the fo'c'sle-head, as the watch prepared to go alongside. The Le Havre pilot was standing aside in the wheelhouse, waiting to help if required and keeping a check on the depth. The officer of the watch was standing-by the the telegraph. The binnacle light projected its eerie green light upon Gaston's worn and leathery face. The navigating officer, who was the second mate, stood facing the doppler log, while he called out the speeds as the master made the approach . . . 'range two thousand three hundred metres, sir . . . *Niger*'s bearing is drawing slowly ahead.'

'Very good. Starboard ten. Nine-o revolutions.'

Gael Le Bihan could see her clearly now; he had taken off his dark glasses when he had reached the bridge, so that his eyes were well adjusted to the night. *Niger* was darkened, with only her warning and navigation lights showing. He was sure of her now: he was 20° abaft her starboard beam.

'Hard-a-starboard . . .' This should be about right, but he was still not certain that she was outside his turning circle.

'Speed five-and-a-half, sir,' from the navigator.

Bir-Hakeim's bows were slipping rapidly across the indistinct horizon.

'Ease to ten. Steady on 120°.' Gaston seldom made a mistake, but, nevertheless, Le Bihan remained close to the rudder indicator.

He could see the figures of pigmy men moving listlessly on the starboard side of *Niger*'s main deck: a Chinese crew, the office had said. He hoped they did not suffer Cape disease worse than a European-manned ship. During the long passage, with little to do, minds atrophied until men seemed incapable of taking definite and rapid decisions. On several occasions, Le Bihan had been forced to send his own men across to a VLCC to help make fast their lines – the VLCC crew had stood there, listlessly watching the heaving lines snaking across.

Bir-Hakeim was closing nicely, her bows level with *Niger*'s quarter, a hundred metres clear but overhauling too fast. He must slow her approach rate.

'Steer 120, seven-o revolutions.'

'One forty metres, sir . . .'

The blare of the telegraph cut the silence. Le Bihan felt the wind on his face as he judged the diminishing distance. *Niger*'s captain stood in the VLCC's starboard wing, quietly passing information through the mike of his R/T:

'My course 120°. My speed four decimal two,' Captain Gratton reported.

'Roger . . .'

The Breton leaned over the side to watch the gap closing between the two monsters. The water seethed and hissed as the slab sides of the two tankers remorselessly compressed the seas between them.

'Stop engine,' Le Bihan rapped. 'Lights on.'

The length of *Niger*'s starboard side gleamed suddenly with light, her plates rust-streaked from the twenty-two-day voyage. *Bir-Hakeim*'s side, towering twenty feet above *Niger*, was gliding steadily ahead.

'*Merde*,' Le Bihan swore beneath his breath. 'Too fast.'

The ship shuddered as the for'd fender squelched.

'Lost steerage way,' the helmsman shouted, a note of anxiety in his report.

The bow swung rapidly to starboard, while the stern swung inwards. Le Bihan saw the headrope snaking across.

'Half astern,' he ordered. 'Hard -a-port.'

If this did not check her, there would be an almighty crunch.

6

CHAPTER 2

ss *Niger Petrola*, VLCC

Thursday, 3 June
Wind: Force 4, wsw
Visibility: 3 miles

'Let go starboard anchor.'

Captain William Gratton leaned over the lip of his starboard wing, watching the mate and his cable party, almost out of sight and nearly quarter of a mile away on the fo'c'sle-head. *Bir-Hakeim* had come alongside harder than he had expected but there had been no spark, no damage, because those Japanese fenders had absorbed most of the shock. As Bill Gratton heard the distant rumble of the chain, he glanced upwards at the small figure of the French captain poised high up in *Bir-Hakeim's* port wing. Gratton did not envy him his job.

'Thanks, Captain. Ready to pump when I've come to my cable.'

The answering shout was lost in the clatter echoing from *Bir-Hakeim's* deck, as the hoses were being slung across on the cranes. Gratton knew that Le Bihan was a cool operator who enjoyed a considerable reputation in Universal's fleet.

The anchor bell was clanging for'd: *Niger* swung to wind and tide and then the hoses were connected. The portable gangway between the ships gleamed beneath the flood lights and he could see *Bir-Hakeim's* white-overalled officers scrambling across to help his own crew with the special connectors. The cranes whined as the jibs elevated to plumb the stirrups; the first hoses went across and the right-angled bend was adjusted until it was abreast *Niger's*

7

manifold. Another overalled figure was wrestling with the massive brass flange; a hand waved in signal and the link was made. The two ships were now joined by their connecting cord, ready to transfer the crude oil.

'Ready to take in cargo . . . Start pumping, Captain, please . . .' Gratton registered Le Bihan's order and waved back his acknowledgement. He glanced over the side to take a final look at the springs. They were bearing an even strain and the ships seemed happy enough.

'Start pumping,' he told his chief officer over the intercom. He saw the sudden pulsation in the huge rubber transfer pipe, as the pumps began discharging. In a few minutes they would be pumping at a hundred tons a minute. To lighten *Niger* by 50,000 tons would take over eight hours. It was already 0240, so that they could not break-away before 1100, even if all went well. He would get his head down now and snatch a few hours sleep; if the forecast of fog persisted, tomorrow would be a long day and he needed to be fresh for the passage through the Straits. He was due at Fredericia at 0900 on Saturday, 5 June, which meant he had little time in hand. Wearily he hauled himself off to his bridge cabin. The sudden demands of the Channel after the soporific haul round the Cape were telling on him. He was tired after the last two nights on the bridge and he knew it.

He reached out for the telephone buzzing by the headboard of his bunk. The clock showed 0450.

'Captain, sir, Second Mate speaking. Fog is shutting down.'

Bill Gratton stifled a yawn and swore softly. 'What's the visibility?'

'About a mile, sir. I am placing the fo'c'sle-head lookout.'

'Thanks. Let me know at once if it gets any worse.' He never had difficulty in sleeping, but morning twilight was already stealing through the chinks in the curtains of his scuttle when he dozed off again. His Chinese steward woke him at seven, and he heard the cup rattle in its saucer as it was laid upon the side table. This was always one of the best moments when Prue and the children seemed closest.

She was an understanding girl and had taken his acceptance of the *Niger* job in good part. She knew that he would enjoy less leave this way, working for his Greek masters under the Liberian flag, than if he stayed with Universal. But the money was good and, as a young captain, he would benefit from the experience: with luck he could reach the top more quickly. At thirty-two he was not doing too badly, but the house and Michael's education were taking too large a share of his income. If it had not been for his father's help, there were times when he had not known how to cope. He, like most sailors, was no good with money, but he had learned at last how to save, once again thanks to his Old Man.

The Grattons had always been a close-knit family, bound together as they had been through generations of seafaring. He wondered if Michael would go to sea, with things as they now were. Twenty-four hour turn-rounds and the interminable slogs to the Gulf and back were unlikely to attract youngsters to sea. If Michael did not take up the profession, he would be the first Gratton for generations not to follow the calling; the family had been sailing out of Liverpool since great-great-grandfather Samuel had been a master-owner holding the king's letter of marque, a treasured family heirloom which father had hung in the hall of their home at Rochester. This sense of family had bound them all together and, when things were difficult, it was great to feel that this bond was there.

It would be good to talk to his father this evening when *Niger* passed through the Straits – Captain Stuart Gratton, Harbour Master, East Thames, was sure to require contact with *Niger* – he never missed a trick and was, Bill recognized, one of the most competent seamen he had met. An extraordinary man, his father: though a practical and experienced mariner, methodical and precise in all that he did, he was a dreamer and a visionary, able to see the far horizon much clearer than most. Whereas most men were adept at their own particular skill and job, father never allowed the trees to obscure his vision of the whole wood. This quality did not always endear him to others, particularly when he wanted his own way. He certainly did not suffer fools gladly, as

9

Bill could remember to his cost – and he smiled to himself as he hauled himself from his bunk.

He moved to the large port overlooking the main deck and twitched back the chintz curtain which Prue had made for him; visibility had certainly shut down – and he felt the twinge of anxiety that had recently begun to give pain in his lower abdomen. He could still see his fo'c'sle-head, but he doubted if visibility was much more than three-quarters of a mile. The bell was ringing regularly and the third mate, a happy-go-lucky Ghanaian, was on the bridge keeping anchor watch.

Bill Gratton yawned. He glared at the unshaven face in the mirror as he grasped his razor – not too bad for thirty-two, but in spite of taking his daily exercise with the Indian clubs, the deck hockey and the swimming, there were already signs that he was losing the battle which they all had to fight: too full in the face; his former robustness, which had stood him in good stead as a front-row prop, was running to paunchy fat; too good and too ample a diet combined with an unnatural existence on board a floating hotel.

The Chinese chefs were excellent, but the food was tending to become monotonous; he would be glad to taste some of Prue's cooking again. The Chinese were a good lot: they worked hard if they were left alone and were allowed to get on with the job. He understood them now, thanks to the guidance of John Bullock, his chief officer, who had served most of his time with Chinese crews. But, if you crossed them, they could be the very devil: obstinate, while simulating incomprehension until they drove you to fury. They always won in the end, as one master had learned to his cost, when one afternoon the entire crew had walked off the ship and demanded to be flown back to Hong Kong. Head Office had not been enthusiastic.

The razor whirred and the stubble disappeared to reveal his sunburnt face. The grey eyes peering back at him from the mirror had been inherited from his long-suffering mother. She had been good to Prue, not obtruding, but gently showing her the way to acceptance of the wife's role when hitched to a sailor. The telephone was ringing again.

'Chief Officer, sir. Visibility is shutting down. Met. report gives thick fog in the Straits. Shall I ask the Chief for steam at immediate notice?'

'Thanks, John. Come to "stand-by". I'll be up in a moment.'

He opened the for'd port and stood motionless for a moment. An uneasiness, a strange presentiment that this was going to be a difficult passage stole through him. He shivered as the clammy coldness of the fog drove through the cabin.

Gratton stood in the wing of *Niger*'s bridge. He was talking down to his opposite number in *Bir-Hakeim*, their positions now being reversed, with Captain Le Bihan looking upwards. It was already 0930 but there were only another 2000 tons to discharge. *Bir-Hakeim* was low in the water and her chief officer was sounding tanks for the last time. Both masters were discussing a small echo that was closing on a steady bearing at speed on the port bow.

'Don't like it, Captain,' Le Bihan said.

'She's 1500 yards from my bridge,' Gratton replied. 'She's not answering my fog-signal . . .' At that instant, *Niger*'s hooter blared again above them, vibrating his ear drums with the resonance: a short blast, followed by a prolonged, then another short.

The Frenchman had disappeared into his wheelhouse. Bill Gratton returned also for another hurried check: the echo was still steady and was now at 1100 yards. He heard Le Bihan shouting at him through his megaphone.

'Are you to your marks, Captain?'

'Yes,' Gratton shouted.

'I'm breaking away . . .' Le Bihan called. Bill saw him yanking at his hooter lever. Six blasts reverberated through the fog now swirling in patches about their ships.

'*Emergency break-away.*' the Frenchman yelled through his megaphone to the white-overalled figure by the crane. As Le Bihan reached his engine room telegraph, the deck hands were racing to their stations.

Gratton darted back to his wheelhouse. 'Warn the engine room,' he ordered. He grabbed the intercom as the first group of

Chinese scrambled towards the manifold. 'Weigh anchor, full speed.'

One of *Bir-Hakeim*'s chief officers was bawling across the gap: '*Break-away*! Shut down. Disconnect the hose . . .'

The fire parties in *Bir-Hakeim* were already manning their hose-guns, some of the hands in their asbestos suits.

Niger's deck party were yanking frenziedly at the huge spanners. The connecting flange rattled on the deck. There was a yell through the fog from *Bir-Hakeim*'s fo'c'sle-head: 'All gone for'd . . . stand by the fore-spring . . .' *Niger*'s hooter blared again, its warning obliterating all else.

Bir-Hakeim's bows were paying off when the gangway between the ships tilted crazily, the white figure of their second officer still clinging to its lattice-work. The crane operator tried to hoist the gangway free from the stirrups which supported the hoses now swinging above the confused water threshing between the ships.

'Let go back-spring . . . let go stern ropes.' Le Bihan was leaning over his port wing, megaphone in hand. As the lightener slowly gathered way and swung outwards, the Frenchman raised his hand.

'*Bon voyage*, Captain . . . I'll drop my pilot and follow you up Channel. I'll lie off and stand-by while you weigh.'

Gratton waved and dashed back to his radar. The anchor bell rang three shackles. Jamming his forehead into the visor, he again identified the echo disappearing into the ground clutter.

'Full ahead on the engine.' By the time the ship had way on, the anchor would be up-and-down and would break free on the turn. 'One prolonged blast . . .'

There was no more that he could do. He held his breath and waited, his eyes sweeping the impenetrable fog that was blanketing the length of his port side. The collision would come from there.

He felt the trembling of the ship's hull as she slowly responded to the revolutions. The hooter blared again; the anchor bell rang its two shackles. The chain rattled for'd as it came in. He could hear the chief officer's voice over the intercom. He was shrouded by the fog but he was in the eyes of the ship, watching the cable coming in. Then suddenly he was yelling at the top of his voice through his loudhailer, the howling of the amplifier drowning the intercom:

'Go to starboard, you bloody fools . . . *To starboard!*'

The ship was moving ahead and the compass card was beginning to swing. Gratton could just distinguish men scrambling down the port side and leaning over the rails. The Chinese bosun was screaming unintelligibly and pointing over the side.

CHAPTER 3

Harbour Master, East Thames

Thursday, 3 June
Wind: Force 3, SSE
Visibility: 6 miles

Captain Stuart Gratton, Harbour Master, East Thames, entered his office, his glance falling from habit upon the tattered parchment flags stuck upon his desk: they had been by him for a long time, since those relatively carefree days when he had been Staff Signals officer at *Dolphin*, the Submarine Base at Gosport. The flags had been presented to him when he had departed for his 'golden bowler'. 'There's always bloody something,' the first read; the other, 'Out of the ashes of today's programme rises the phoenix of tomorrow's foul-up.' Even a sour grimace was beyond him today.

He had spent a gruelling morning at a meeting with shipping people in the offices of the Port of London Authority. For three hours his companions had been trying to convince the majority that safety in the Thames could come about only through order and conformity imposed upon those who wished to navigate these waters; that order and conformity depended upon an agreed procedure, simple and understandable, even by foreigners; and that procedure could evolve only through long and patient discussion.

Gratton was beginning to feel his years. This was the first moment since he had taken on this job that he had thought of unloading the responsibility for overseeing the safe and timely arrival of ships to their various billets in the Thames. For fifteen years he had been trying to transform an archaic system into an organization that could cope with deep-draught ships and modern conditions. After this morning's battle, he wondered whether the effort was worth it: the constant strain of fighting hide-bound attitudes and of coping with the remorseless queue of ships waiting in the estuary – and of sailing them again – was beginning to affect his health.

His game leg did not help, particularly with his weight and height – over six-foot-three. The damage to his hip after the mining in *Esk* had left him with a permanent limp; he had always managed but now the other leg was giving trouble – arthritis in the other hip had begun its insidious invasion. He had asked Judy to give him sandwiches this morning because he needed a few minutes' peace in his office during the lunch hour, whilst the non-watchkeepers were taking their break – and Bill might tele-phone from his new ship on his way through the Straits to Fredericia.

Judy had shown concern for Stuart as he had left their house in Rochester that morning. 'Take care of yourself, Shorty,' she had said as she kissed him (he'd never been able to shake off the tag since *Worcester* days). 'You're working too hard. Stop being selfish, dear . . . You've got me to think of too.' Her unusual out-burst had started him thinking, as he had fought his way in the commuter train up to town and the PLA offices. He was thankful to be back here on the river again, in the centre of things at the headquarters of the Thames Navigation Service in Gravesend.

Cucumber and brown bread – and the Burton's bottle . . . what more could he ask? But was he really beginning to look as old as he sometimes felt? He limped towards the window in his office, a spacious room giving a direct view down river to Shornmead and Coalhouse Forts and the Lower Hope. He paused by the small mirror near the door: certainly, his brown hair was silvering rapidly and was thinning on top; true, the crowsfeet at the corners of his eyes were more deeply etched, the crescent lines at the corners of his wide mouth more sarcastic than once they had been; perhaps, also, the hollows in his leathery cheeks were more prominent and his neck scraggier, but there was still fire in his belly and the grey of his eyes was still clear.

The Harbour Master had to be prepared to fight, if he was to be any good – tomorrow's movements merely proved the force of his argument. The tides were falling off and high water was not until 1900. There was a big container ship to sail from Tilbury dock and the VLCC from Universal Port Terminal, but the container could not be clear of Tilbury Lock until the evening tide because of yesterday's walkout by the crane teams – and the VLCC would not have discharged before then. As soon as he had them dispatched and down-river, and it was safe for the inward boys to come up, he would berth Universal's lightener first . . . he glanced at the movements' list: *Bir-Hakeim*, 80,000 tons; if the tide made as predicted, she would have eighteen inches under her on arrival off the berth. Her master was a Frenchman who knew his stuff; he had been up to Universal several times since the lightening game had started. Ships like her were no problem.

Though the outer limits of the PLA extended almost to the Tongue Light Vessel, it was the pressure of the mounting queues in the Tongue and the Southend and Warp deep-water anchorages that worried him. How the devil could he organize a smooth traffic flow up to London, if he did not know what was pouring through the Straits? 'Like a farm track swamped with motorway traffic,' Bill Beavis had described the Dover Straits in the press.

The ships which eventually debouched into Stuart's patch were still not adequately controlled, in spite of his and his friends' earlier triumph over convention. That struggle had been the most exhausting battle of all, having been defeated by sheer weight of tradition in their attempts to control movement, after the passing of The Harbours Act in 1964. Authority had finally succeeded, in a private Act in 1968. With the help of the oilmen, it had achieved what it needed through 'The Powers of General and Special Directions', enabled by The Harbours Act. History had been made and other ports had followed their lead.

Previously, if a ship so wished, she could steam up to Tower Bridge which would be opened for her, in spite of halting the New Cross-City traffic. She could immediately turn round and proceed to sea again, provided her Master had entered her at the Custom House and complied with the By-Laws. There was no compulsion for her to report her plans beforehand.

The Harbour Master returned to his desk as the phone pealed.

'Captain Gratton . . . ? North Foreland Radio here, sir. Will you be available to take a link call from *Niger Petrola*? She's turn number three, but we thought you'd like to know in case you have to leave your office.'

'Thanks. I'm available . . . good of you.'

They were a pleasant lot, down there. He had made friends with them long ago when he had been setting up the communications and broadcast arrangements. You could have anything you wanted these days, provided you had the money. With the scanner at Warden Point on the Isle of Sheppey, the radar coverage of the estuary and sea reaches was excellent. The signal was relayed by microwave via Southend to his displays here at the operations centre, alongside those from the up-river radars.

It was thoughtful of Bill to ring – the call would be through in about fifteen minutes. He chewed his sandwiches as he glanced at tomorrow's Movement Programme: *Outward:* he knew all about them . . . *Inward: Bir-Hakeim*; a couple of big container ships; assorted medium-sized cargo carriers; *Pollux*, another container ship with notorious old Braydon Fancourt as master; a Chilean destroyer on a courtesy visit to London; the Russian grain-carrier, *Yalta*, for the Northfleet Hope grain terminal; and the Japanese bulk cement-carrier, *Awa Maru*, for Bevan's Jetty. That was enough for one high water, but they could not be allowed up until Universal's VLCC had been turned and sailed from their new terminal.

Thank God he had a far-sighted Authority. At least the outward container from Tilbury would know that several cargo carriers would be on their way down from London on the ebb and, thanks again to the Movements Programme, they would realize also that the container ship would be backing out from the Tilbury lock at the same time. Incredible to believe that London had wanted to scotch the Movements Programme idea.

It was the 1966 Seaman's strike which had done the trick. The uncontrolled congestion, with inward ships piling up in the docks, had impelled the owners to ask for help. The Authority had insisted, then, that the owners should inform a central control centre of their ship's expected movements and of their intentions, both 'in' and 'out'; the Harbour Authority also made the owners promise that they would do what was asked of them. They co-operated admirably and so the monitoring system had been born.

For the first time, Stuart Gratton had known what ships would be coming up. Since then, using the powers of the General Directions, the development of the monitoring system had evolved naturally and swiftly. It had been 'All systems, Go,' in spite of the intense opposition from the traditionalists who continued to insist that the Master must remain, even in these exciting and fast-moving days, responsible only to himself.

The phone was shrilling.

'North Foreland here, sir. I've spoken to *Niger Petrola*'s radio officer: they've just entered thick fog and the captain can't leave the bridge.'

'Any message?'

'The captain said he'd ring you later, when things ease up a bit. Sorry about that, sir.'

'Okay. Thanks for trying.'

Stuart Gratton felt a glow of satisfaction. He'd brought up his son with the mariner's traditional caution. Bill would not risk the safety of his ship, and hazard others, because of external pressures from schedules and owners. He was also acquiring a growing appreciation of the master's role in supporting the demands of modern traffic schemes.

'Thank you, Captain Gratton.' North Foreland was signing off. 'Nice to hear you. Good afternoon.'

The Harbour Master put down the phone, scraped back his chair and moved across to open the window. It was slack water and the dark ribbon of the Thames curled peacefully towards the estuary. He shivered from the sudden chill in the air: it would be hazy across the marshes – there was fog about and it would soon be in the lower reaches.

CHAPTER 4

ss *Maori Frigo, Container Ship*

Thursday, 3 June
Wind: Force 2, NE
Visibility: 1 cable

'Thanks for standing by us, Pilot.'

Captain Thirsk shook hands with the Belgian and watched the man slowly descending the bridge ladder. The pilot had been worried by the tug incident when turning *Maori* in Zeebrugge harbour. The Belgian had underestimated the power of the container ship's bow thrusters and had girted the tug – the little vessel had let go her tow in the nick of time; her gunwale was awash when she slipped the warp. Thirsk walked to the starboard bridge wing and picked up the phone to *Maori*'s fo'c'sle-head.

'Weigh.'

The clanking of the chain echoed through the fog now enveloping the forepart of his ship; her bows, even if the day had been clear, would have been invisible because of the container boxes stacked four high on the upper deck. The horn from the Zeebrugge breakwater was moaning its dismal warning from somewhere on his starboard quarter. There were a few minutes left for him to consider the last leg of the voyage lying before him – this final lap, after the nine-week voyage to New Zealand and back.

Maori Frigo was a fine ship. Her paintwork and her spotless engine room did not betray the three years which she had been working non-stop, except for docking. She was the second of her class, the result of years of planning: the container revolution and its attendant world-wide capital investment had ruthlessly by-passed the laggard shipping companies.

She carried over a thousand container boxes. Calling at container berths en route to New Zealand – Europe, America, Australia – she unloaded, picked up and sailed to a strict schedule. If there were no boxes ready for her – hard luck. Hers was a delivery and pick-up service and she had to be slotted into the pre-booked container crane berths which had been established around the globe.

Shipowners were in this business to make money: the massive investment was geared to the concept of container ship, container berth, container off-loading on to road lorries or container freight trains – the operation had to be international. Trade ignored frontiers. The Russians and their satellites were in the game; they could not afford to be left in the cold.

Displacing 40,000 tons, *Maori Frigo* was the ultimate in refrigerated container ships. She drew over thirty feet when fully loaded and, with her Babcock and Wilcox boilers and huge propellers, she could knock up twenty-eight knots at full speed. The round trip to New Zealand took seven weeks, but she was replacing the equivalent of six traditional cargo ships which had previously served the same refrigerated run. The cost was high: if she remained idle in port, her running costs were £3000 an hour. She could burn over 400 tons of oil fuel a day at full speed.

'Thruster' Thirsk was proud of his ship, but this modern concept of ship-management was not to his taste. He had gone to sea for the excitement, but the romance vanished with the accountants, computers and the container revolution. Seeing the world was now a matter of calling at similar container berths where the huge cranes existed, discharge and load, and off to sea for the next depot, without the chance of a run-ashore for the crew.

Zeebrugge, from which he had sailed two hours ago, was a fair example. This Belgian port which had grown so rapidly because of its efficiency, could have been a good run for the lads, because of the holiday atmosphere at neighbouring Blankenberghe and the proximity of Ostend. But the discharge and the working of the ship took priority, because she was already six hours astern of schedule, owing to the lightning stoppage of labour at Tilbury yesterday morning.

Maori had been loading to catch the nine o'clock tide. She had only a few more boxes to stow at 0800, the shifts having been working all night to finish the job. Thirsk had been surprised, and then angry, when at 0810 the cranes were still motionless: the morning shift had walked out because of a minor organizational problem over the working of the quay and the straddlers, those yellow beetles, monstrous in size and grotesque in shape, which shifted the boxes from beneath the cranes to the stacks in various corners of the compound. Even the refrigerated containers were taken care of: they were transported by the diesel-driven four-wheeled straddlers to the transverse lines of cooler units on the wharf. Each cold container was connected to a unit which blew cold air into the box while it waited for its refrigerated lorry.

Thruster had no illusion as to his own character: he was impatient, restless and voracious for knowledge and fresh experience. He did not suffer fools gladly and knew that his young officers considered him eccentric – and certainly he held that reputation at Head Office. He had earned his nickname from the days when he was still third mate and went ballooning during his leaves. On one of his last flights, the balloon had drifted too far to leeward and had landed in a field, the only other occupant being a pedigree bull, Thruster of Banbury. Whilst Third Mate Thirsk was unravelling himself from the mess, the bull decided to charge this unheralded visitor from space; in the fracas, Alexander Thirsk had received a gash across his cheek which had left an ugly scar. The press had made hay of the story; his messmates had dubbed him 'Thruster'; and, to conceal the scar, he had worn his bushy red beard ever since. The Thirsks were Lancashire folk, which was another reason why the call of Liverpool was so strong at the moment. The anchor bell rang out its two shackles and he turned to the third mate standing-by in the wheelhouse.

'Slow ahead, port twenty.'

He could not help but compare the efficiency of Zeebrugge with the situation at Tilbury. Two crane drivers and one supervisor

21

in the small Belgian port; he had counted over fourteen men trying to look busy when doing the same job at Tilbury. The British crane operators and the straddler drivers certainly worked hard but, apart from the charge-hand, known as the shift manager, and the checker, there were too many idlers with nothing to do – what a sad and vicious circle all this was. There could be only one result: Southampton was the best example of which he could think.

That huge port, where King Canute had done his stuff, had committed suicide. Southampton was dead in comparison with its competitors across the Channel. And tomorrow, he supposed, Liverpool was likely to be in the same dismal state; the agents had warned him that *Maori* could be held up, because the Birkenhead dockies were driving round in buses to Liverpool docks in an effort to win support. Two men, it seemed, were required to operate a crane; in Liverpool, six men were allocated, two to drive, four to drink in the local. Birkenhead was allowed only four – and so the cranemen felt aggrieved: they were on strike and bringing the docks to a standstill because they were demanding an extra two drivers. So far, they had failed to bring out the Liverpool men – there were signs that the good sense of the British working-man was at last overcoming the blandishments of the trouble-makers, but the awakening was a long time coming.

Surprisingly, the New Zealand dockies were even worse – they had held ships up for weeks. Modern costs could not accept these stupid extravagances which was why our ports were dying. Until we sorted ourselves out and accepted the hard facts of economic life, we would continue to sink. How could a nation survive in a free market, when it paid young unskilled labourers £50 a week for sitting on their backsides in the docks? The slide into bankruptcy was inevitable, when management never communicated in human terms with the men who worked the docks. Without communication, human relations soured. He wondered how much longer the Liver birds would continue to watch over Liverpool from their twin towers on the Liver buildings. According to legend, when Liverpool died, the Liver birds would take off.

The fo'c'sle-head bell sounded again: anchor up-and-down. Captain Thirsk moved to the starboard wing and watched the water curling along the side. The ship was down to her marks and, in this anchorage close to Zand buoy, she had to be under way by 1400 if she was to be comfortable when crossing the ten fathom line at Ostend Bank North buoy. From then onwards, to the separation line at West Hinder, there was plenty of water.

'Anchor's aweigh, sir.'

The first mate's voice was reassuring over the intercom. He and the second mate were the only fully certificated officers, other than Thirsk. The third mate, though keen and sensible, was inexperienced and held no ticket. Thruster had complained to Head Office, but there were no watchkeepers to be found – and this was the state to which his revered service had been brought by modern conditions. It was dishonest luring young men to sea by the romance of the game; the only alternative was money. Officers were paid well – but, thank God, youth today needed a purpose more satisfying. The job had to be worthwhile as well as exciting.

The shortage of officers had led to extraordinary anomalies: a master could no longer hide behind the facade of Captain Bligh. Today's officer had to be asked, not told – Thruster had choked when he had overheard the third mate telephoning the engine room . . . 'We'd be most grateful if you could give us a bit more . . .'

Captain Thirsk called across to the second mate:

'Let's come round to 257°, shall we? Ninety revolutions.'

Thruster had tried everything, but even his sarcasm had not broken down this modern attitude. Perhaps there was no harm in it, but he disliked the trend. Familiarity did cause trouble: all went well until a senior man had to deliver a reprimand – and a junior officer liked to know where he stood.

The captain strode back into the wheelhouse and stooped over the serviceable radar: Sparks, a twenty-three-year-old, whilst trying to service the main set, had succeeded in putting it out of action. All that could be seen of the radar was a mass of tools at the pedestal foot, whilst the worried, pale-faced radio officer tinkered with its guts as he glared at the handbook. Thruster bit back his sarcasm: this promised to be a memorable twenty-four hours, if the Channel fog persisted round Land's End to Liverpool.

The Zand buoy showed clearly and close to starboard; Ostend Bank North was coming up and, once he had found it, he would increase to eighteen knots if there was little traffic. He preferred to maintain speed when crossing the lanes, to cut down the time in the hazardous area – with this modern radar and relative-tracking, provided both were used and appreciated properly, the practice was justifiable.

After checking that the new officer of the watch and helmsman were happy on the new course, he moved out again to the bridge wing. Under-officered he certainly was, for there were times during this voyage when he had had to keep a watch himself; and the inexperience of his officers was aggravated by the change-over that had taken place at Tilbury. Half the crew and a third of his officers had been relieved by these new faces who had joined for the next four voyages. The man on the wheel at the moment had never before encountered this type of hand steering; he had already once chased the card round. Thruster had only avoided putting the ship on the mud by instinctive reaction to the apparent shift in the relative wind (the fog horizon was formless). He had managed to bring the helmsman back, before the ship charged out of this treacherous, wreck-strewn channel at the mouth of the Scheldt.

Thirsk could hear the whistle of the Wenduine buoy, faint on his port bow. In a few moments he would alter up to the Akkaert Middle buoy; then he would set course for the West Hinder. He hated fog more than any other hazard – this thick, soupy stuff, dirty yellow as it swirled across the length of his ship, lent little charm to the ochre sea skirting these low-lying dunes. He felt exhilarated by the challenge of this passage, but he knew only too well the reaction that would swamp him when he reached the south-west-bound lane. He was tired after these night passages up-channel, into the Thames, then sailing again yesterday, across to Belgium.

He had snatched some sleep, in spite of the Zeebrugge dredgers

that had been clanking away all night. He would be glad to reach
Liverpool and hand over to Jack Filey, the relief master. *Maori*
might yet make up the time lost at Tilbury, but, if the fog persisted, there was no hope. He would not allow his judgement to
be influenced by outside pressures – even by the owners' dis-
pleasure at missing a pre-booked berth.

God help the shipmasters when, and if ever, zonal control of
shipping was adopted. This procedure was already working in
the re-opened Suez Canal – a thirty-three-knot container ship
considered that her running entry into the canal began at
Gibraltar. A pre-booked slot was awaiting her and she had to be
there on time, prepared for immediate entry. These expensive
ships could no longer waste time in anchorages.

When zonal control materialized, the shipmaster would have to
accept control by the shore authorities. For some of the idiots at
sea today, direction was essential. As far as he, Alexander Thirsk,
was concerned, the development could not come quickly enough.
If the seafaring brotherhood did not adapt themselves, sociology
and the politics of the environmentalists would impose direction
through the force of law. Air traffic control had been brought
about by the immediacy of the air-transport explosion. The same
pressures were at work today upon the movements of shipping
through congested water-space.

'Course, sir, 287°.'

The ship was clear of the worst stretch, the shallows and the
Wandelaar wrecks. Thirsk sighed and again checked the rudder
repeat-indicator. He felt the wind in his face but his eyes were
already feeling the strain as he peered into the bright glare of the
fog. A few hours of this and he would be seeing shapes looming
at him from every point of the compass. So far so good; apart
from one echo crossing the south side of the separation line, the
route was clear to the West Hinder lightship.

'May I come round now, sir?' the second mate asked from the
chart table.

'A1 whistle buoy is abeam to port, half a mile.'

'Yes, but nothing to starboard. We're close enough to the
Akkaert bank. Come ten degrees to port.'

As Captain Thirsk crouched again over the radar visor, he called out to the officer of the watch.

'Keep your eyes skinned. And watch your ship's head. There's a group of fishing craft ahead. Start the hooter.'

As he raised his head from the black visor, the resonance from the low boom of the fog hooter set his ears on edge. He would get across this bit as rapidly as he could – then on to the south-west lane. If there were no rogues about, the day might not be so bloody after all.

He checked the time by the bridge clock. It was showing 1352.

CHAPTER 5

MV *Ypres,*
Cross Channel Ferry

Thursday, 3 June
Wind: Force 2, NE
Visibility: 1 cable (200 yards)

Ostend Airport:

Guy Hannen swung the Volkswagen off to the right, thankful to be leaving the autoroute down which he had been flogging since leaving the camp site at ten to five this morning. Ella, his Canadian wife and eight years younger, had been patient with the children who, on the whole, had been remarkably good during their family marathon across Europe. But, with the thought of returning to the problems of his taxi firm, he was beginning to feel his thirty-eight years. If it had not been for Peter, his younger brother who was holding the fort for him, he would never have been able to get away – the last minute rush of passports, tickets and air bookings, insurance and green cards, anti-typhoid jabs and all the rest, had left Ella and him gasping. They had needed a week to unwind, but now he could face the coming year with less apprehension.

'There it is,' Ella shouted above the engine. 'Airport and Carflights Airways: keep to your right for departures.'

'Thanks, dear. Have everything ready.' He could see her fumbling with the folder, searching for the tickets.

The drive back to the Channel coast had been the worst part of the whole holiday – mist and fog becoming denser all the way. Passing Bruges he had been forced to ease down to a crawl. Here at Ostend it was still bloody thick and he did not care for flying in these conditions – not after his short spell as a pilot in the Navy, when there had been a Fleet Air Arm . . . those had been desperate days, when he had been pushed out with a golden bowler. At least he was his own boss now, though this was no sinecure for the small private enterprise man in modern Britain. The road widened before him and the tower loomed from out of the mist. Visibility was fifty yards on the runways.

At the arrivals desk, he was informed that all traffic was suspended temporarily: the first flight might take off about noon if conditions did not worsen. Apparently, visibility on the other side in Kent was as bad as here in Ostend.

'Even if they were operating in this,' he said to Ella when he rejoined her, 'I'd cancel the booking. They'll have to refund our fares. We'll try the sea ferries and find out if we can get the car on board. I'll come back here and cancel.'

The Belgian car ferry, *Ypres*, offered a vacancy which Hannen immediately took. There were no cabins, but four couchettes were still available, though separated. Her sailing had been delayed until two o'clock, so that they had plenty of time in which to cancel their air bookings. By 1210 the Volkswagen had joined the queue for boarding *Ypres*. There ensued the usual flap of passport presentations and custom clearance. Ella seemed to work herself up into a stew over these formalities: he tried to keep his patience as she let him have the rough edge of her tongue.

At 1245 the first of the cars trundled into the gaping car deck. Hannen drove over the ramp, his overhead rack just clearing the deckhead, following an unintelligible remonstrance with a three-striped Belgian officer who sported a drooping, Mexican moustache. The long flaxen hair sprouting beneath the man's cap seemed ridiculous to Hannen, but he was irritable and unjustifiably critical of his fellow men this morning. He was lucky to have obtained a booking; a ship felt much safer in fog than a plane. A ship could always anchor . . .

The cleaners were still mopping up in the passages and there was a smell of vomit in the lavatories to which he had taken his nine-year-old, Mark. The steward explained that the ship had been held up in the fog off Dover and that the swell had upset the passengers. The man's graphic gestures had silenced Mark's effusiveness.

Hannen waited in the passageway for Ella and their five-year-old Lucy, and then they found their reclining seats on the port side of 'c' deck. After prolonged discussion it was decided that Mark would look after his mother in one pair of seats, while he and Lucy occupied the other, about ten rows ahead. Lucy established herself firmly by the huge square window, while he stowed the hand baggage in the rack at the end of the passage. All this fuss bothered him these days: females seemed incapable of accepting these details as unimportant. He needed a few moment's peace, if he were not to blow his top.

'Coming on deck, Ella, to watch her sail?'

'Lucy's almost asleep. I'll stay with her.'

'I want to see the boat. Come on, Dad.' Mark was tugging at his hand and together they wound their way through the milling throng that was scrambling to grab the best seats before the ship sailed. Already groups were forming outside the duty-free shops, the girls outside the perfumery, the men in front of the booze and cigarette grilles that were closed until the ship was clear of territorial waters. Guy Hannen and his son wound their way up the central stairway to the top deck.

'That's better.' Guy felt the clammy cold of the fog and slipped on the greasy wetness of the deck. He led Mark to a gap between the lifeboats where they leaned across the rail to watch the arrival of the shore gangs.

'What's this, Dad?' His son was touching one of the white, fibre-glass cylinders which was lashed and toggled to its slipway.

'Life-rafts. You pull that cord and the whole thing slips into the water. There's a rubber raft inside which inflates itself automatically.'

'If the boat goes down?'

'If the ship's sinking – but the captain has to order "Abandon Ship" first. Come on, let's have a look round.' Together they strolled aft and leaned over the athwartships. The upper poop deck, open to the elements, was packed with container lorries.

Hannen counted six of them, while sailors in blue overalls secured the chassis of the last lorry on the port side; the driver watched with critical interest as the chain hooks were snapped home.

'They tie them down like that in case of bad weather,' Guy said. 'No trouble this trip, Mark; with this fog, we'll have a flat calm all the way.' A Belgian officer, a man of about twenty-five with two stripes on his shoulder badges, smiled as he clambered towards them up the starboard ladder, a chart under his arm.

'Sorry for the delay, sir,' he said in excellent English. 'Had a bit of trouble ashore.'

Hannen raised his eyebrows. 'So long as we reach Dover this evening, that's all that matters. I have to work tomorrow.'

'One of the fork trucks broke down: a shackle sheared and that has held up the loading. The captain wants to wait a bit, anyhow, to give the fog a chance to clear, so we won't have lost too much time.' He grinned: 'I've snatched an extra hour's sleep, so I don't mind.' He leaned on the rail beside them and seemed inclined to talk.

'What's your job in the ship?' Guy asked.

'Second Mate. I look after the navigation.'

'Boring, with the continuous running, day-in, day-out?'

The officer shook his head. 'No voyage is ever the same. Take this trip: we berthed only two hours ago – we had bother with a fleet of fishing boats off the Outer Ratel banks. We were pushed, in this fog, to keep our schedule, but the Old Man knows the run blindfold; he's been doing it for eight years. He smells his way about – hardly needs the radars . . .' The second mate laughed, and his pale, thin face lit up. 'We've got the most modern equipment of all the ferries – computer, relative tracking, the lot.'

'Doesn't fog bother you, crossing the shipping lanes?'

The navigator hesitated, then unrolling the chart and spreading it upon the lid of the lifebuoy locker, traced with his finger the Channel shipping routes. 'We ferries tend to look after ourselves, but it's difficult for other ships to realize that we are entirely in control of the situation. It would be easier if we could hoist a signal telling them to disregard our own motions. But that's a long way off, with the slowness of international agreement at sea. We'd prefer not to have fog – take today's trip . . .'

'What of it?'

'Because of the fishing fleet we encountered on our way in, the captain has decided to cross to Dover via the West Hinder lightship. He'll keep between the Kwinte and Middelkerke banks.' He pointed to the banks off the Belgian coast. 'He'll cut across to the North Bergues buoy, south of the lightship, so we won't have to cross the shipping lanes. We'll stay outside the north-east lane, passing close down the Ruytingen banks. We'll cross the lanes at Sandettié.'

'It's good to see a chart again,' Hannen said. 'I was once in the Navy.'

'I thought you were a sailor, sir, so I thought you'd be interested – so many passengers treat us as bus conductors. We get little thanks.' He shook hands. 'We'll be sailing in a few minutes.'

'By the way, what's your name?'

'Jules van Dyck. Look out for me if you cross with us again.' He saluted and hurried towards the bridge. Minutes later, Guy pointed out to his son the eyes of the warps plopping into the brown waters of the dock. The ship trembled as the bow thrusters pushed her from the jetty. She drew rapidly ahead and the siren blared above their heads.

They stayed on deck until the ferry had cleared the breakwater. There was nothing to see as she nosed out into the fog, so they went below. Lucy was asleep, her head nestled into Ella's shoulder. His long-legged wife smiled up at him, eased from the seat and tucked her daughter into the blanket.

'Look after Mum,' Hannen said to his son. 'Tell her to get some sleep, Mark. We've a long day ahead.'

Ella's lips brushed his cheek as she squeezed past him to find her and Mark's couchettes. He watched them as, settling into their seats behind him, Mark tucked the blanket about his mother's shoulders. Guy Hannen felt the tiredness seeping through his legs while he relaxed into his couchette beside his daughter.

Little Lucy was well away and he stroked her blonde curls. He felt strangely restless and found his thoughts wandering. He watched a couple, two seats ahead of him, one a pale-faced, tired-looking girl of no particular beauty, the other a darkly coloured man, a Tongan by the look of him. The look of tenderness that passed between them was touching to witness, they were so captivated by each other. On their right, a woman in her forties, attractive in her brittle way, with her greying hair curling about her face, sat smoking and staring ahead of her, her thoughts far away; lonely she seemed, wistful . . . every face told its story.

His eyes travelled to the notice painted in two languages across the passage intersection. In French first, then underneath, in English:

IN THE EVENT OF AN EMERGENCY
Passengers must obtain life-jackets and
follow. Arrows leading to assembly stations.

The sign writer could not even get the punctuation right. Underneath was another notice, with a red arrow pointing forwards along the passageway: *To Assembly Station.*

He sat there, his mind uneasy. People were still milling about, unable to find a seat. A crowd of schoolchildren were rushing down the passages, chasing each other and squealing. The Snacks saloon was issuing the last announcement that its service would be closing until four o'clock. The Passport man was ready, the Immigration people were now happy to interview intending travellers to Britain and currency could be exchanged at the Purser's office. The duty-free shop would be opening in half-an-hour's time – it was impossible to sleep. As head of his family, and being an inquisitive creature, he wanted to see for himself where the red arrows led and where the life-saving gear was stowed. He felt beneath the seat for his lifejacket – nothing there. Leaving Lucy sleeping, he stole from his place and eased himself into the passageway.

He moved towards the main stairway and sensed the vibration beneath his feet as the ship picked up speed. She must be outside now, feeling her way through the fog. Six o'clock, Dover, the navigator had said, provided visibility improved. From somewhere above him, faintly, he heard her hooter. He glanced at his watch: 1432 – three and a half hours to go. They would be home by ten.

Second Mate Jules van Dyck marked his latest radar fix on Admiralty chart number 1872. He would now have to transfer this position to the smaller scale, *Dover Strait*. Captain Vanderhaguen insisted on using British charts, but the corrections came in so fast that van Dyck had difficulty in coping. Last February, an average of eight buoys per week had been unlit; and six off-station, three of them over a mile. He slid the chart beneath the other and transferred the position – 126° West Hinder lightvessel 7.2 miles. Alongside the circle, he pencilled the time: 1532. He stood aside as he felt the familiar presence of the captain leaning beside him over the chart table.

'Bring her round to port, to 238°,' Captain Paul Vanderhaguen called to the officer of the watch. 'Reduce to twelve knots.'

Van Dyck felt the vibration decreasing as the ship eased her revolutions. The chief would appreciate the reduction, if no one else. His engines always overheated when crossing the banks and his engine room staff could not cope with any more work at the moment. Because of a two month strike in the shipyard, his department was hard put to it keeping things going: the port cylinder-head gaskets were blowing and the engine room was filthy. But this reduction to twelve knots was unusually large for Vanderhaguen.

Van Dyck glanced surreptitiously at his captain: forty-nine years old, he was the best of the company's masters. He knew the Dover run backwards, having been a ferry skipper for thirteen years, eight of them in *Ypres*. The stubby figure crouching over the chart stooped more than it used to; like all of them, the Old Man was tired and longing for his summer leave. It was always like this, the worst fog month coming at the end of the working year. Vanderhaguen rarely accepted being late for the Dover arrival.

'I'll cross at Sandettié, Pilot.'

Amusement lurked in Vanderhaguen's face as he looked up

at his navigator. The crowsfeet at the corners of his hard, blue eyes were wrinkled with humour and, with that mannerism of his, he tweaked the black beret he wore when they cleared port. Once at sea, he always discarded his uniform and relaxed in his darned maroon sweater; smoking his foul pipe, he would settle into his chair at the corner of the bridge and leave the routine work to his officers. Only when the fog was thick, or if *Ypres* were passing close to the big stuff, did he assume physical command.

'Keep her on this course until we're a mile from Outer Ruytingen West. Let me know when we get there. We're well out of the north-east bound lane, so we should be clear of anything coming up – provided you don't put me on the bank.' Those amused eyes were laughing at Jules's discomfiture, as they peered from below the sandy eyebrows. Vanderhaguen's forehead was lined from the worry of these waters, but the stocky figure slid from the chart table and moved briskly towards the radar. 'The mate's coming up, isn't he? I thought he had the twelve-to-four?'

'Yes, sir. He's finishing his report on the fork-lift breakdown. He asked me to tell you – the office want it in quintuplicate.'

As Vanderhaguen snorted in disgust (he nursed a pathological hatred for bureaucracy) the door at the rear of the wheelhouse slammed. The mate strolled across to the window in front of the helmsman.

'She's all yours, Chief Officer,' Vanderhaguen said. 'As soon as you've taken over, I'll be in my cabin.'

'Right, sir. Fog's thick.'

'I've come down to twelve. You won't need your box of tricks yet . . .'

The third mate turned over the watch and the mate was on his own. He moved over to the radar, then to his pride and joy, the computer-based radar anti-collision machine, the Trumaster, which had been installed by the company. This expensive box of tricks displayed all echoes of ships within a chosen range; it recorded, tracked, then forecast their true and relative courses and speeds. Finally, it selected echoes that were potential collision risks. It indicated the priority of danger, then proposed the course and speed for *Ypres* to avoid collision. It could determine stopped targets; as a final refinement, a warning buzzer warned of approaching collisions when the target was still six miles distant. Vanderhaguen hated it.

To be fair to the Old Man (and van Dyck sympathized with him), the Trumaster had once produced a wrong answer – and once was enough, as far as the Master of the ship was concerned. Total reliance or nothing – the lives of those milling holiday-makers on board were his responsibility. Vanderhaguen preferred to command the ship himself and he mistrusted the machine which an international company was ruthlessly trying to market against world competition.

The mate had resumed his place by the wheel which was now on auto-pilot; the quartermaster was in the wings standing lookout; van Dyck peered once more into the radar: there were five ships coming up from the south-westward – and a large echo which had been worrying him for the past twenty minutes, bore 282°, four to five miles. There was a cluster of small echoes (probably a fishing fleet) three miles to the northward, but these were passing down *Ypres*'s starboard quarter. The big ship had dropped down in speed, worried perhaps by the fishermen – she was proceeding slowly westwards and was obviously making for the south-west lane.

'Nothing to worry about, Pilot,' the mate said, 'Trumaster's got it all wrapped up. This lot coming up through the Straits will pass well clear, the nearest at just under a mile.'

The chief officer was smiling with satisfaction. He was a pro-duct of the new school of officer, wedded to electronics, and Jules found it difficult to like him. He was too good at passing all the paperwork to his juniors and was basically lazy. His black hair was too long and looked slovenly beneath his cap. He resented his duties as car deck officer and at having to spend so much time shepherding the touchy holiday drivers into their parking areas. ('I must be the highest paid car park attendant in the world,' he habitually introduced himself when meeting new faces.) Fortun-ately, the fork-lift incident had been his responsibility and he could not shirk the inevitable report to the office.

'I was checking the large echo to the west of us,' van Dyck said.

'She's out of Zeebrugge and probably south-west bound. She's eased right down.'

'One of the container ships. We've overtaken her; her bearing is passing well clear. How about a coffee, Pilot? We've got a couple of hours before Sandettié.'

Jules van Dyck did not reply. He crossed to the side table at the rear of the wheelhouse, where he switched on the kettle standing amongst the crockery on the tray. The chief was too self-confident: it was not so long ago that he had experienced a near-miss when rounding up for the Ostend entrance. The ship had reported her arrival, when a small coaster, assuming that her voyage was also terminated, disregarded all the rules and blindly turned up across *Ypres*'s bows – they had missed by metres.

The chief officer expected command of a ferry when the Old Man retired. He had better learn humility, or he'd be caught out one of these days.

CHAPTER 6

MV *Castello de Sierra*, Coaster

Thursday, 3 June
Wind: Force 2, NE
Visibility: 550 yards

He felt that he had been conned into this job . . . why had no one told him that the Channel could be like this? But Gonzales Zapiola, Master of the 940-ton coaster, 180 feet long and drawing fourteen feet, felt no resentment on this peaceful afternoon: flat calm, hot sun behind the fog, he revelled in the humidity – and he had spent an uproarious twenty-four hours in Boulogne. The scrap had been loaded and he had sailed from the outer port more or less on time. *Castello de Sierra*, this pig of a ship, had cleared the outer breakwater by 1440 and had rounded the outer whistle buoy at 1507. She was on 'George', the auto-pilot, but he had kept Adolfo, the twelve-to-four helmsman, in the wheelhouse – 'George' had been giving trouble on the way down from Hamburg.

He could not care less this afternoon. He had eaten well in the little restaurant at the back of the quay – the wine (three bottles Janine had shared with him) had been good. And it would be some time before he forgot the woman whose reputation traversed the seven seas – they had recommended her at Hamburg – she was expensive but the money meant little to him, with the way his Greek masters were paying him. No, Gonzales Zapiola beamed to himself, this wasn't a bad life: bloody sight better than if he had stayed in the *Armada Republica Argentina*.

37

The master of *Castello de Sierra* felt happily confused as he staggered through the starboard wheelhouse door – if he stood in the wing, he might hear the siren from Cap Gris Nez. His ancient radar had not been working properly for weeks, but that again was not his responsibility. His Greek masters had insisted on signing on this useless and drunken radio operator and on installing the radar only to satisfy the insurers – not that good equipment made much difference to the premiums. The insurance companies charged as much for ships fitted with ultra-modern gear as for clapped-out old tramps like this, with her obsolescent and minimal equipment.

Cristos, what a night Janine had given him: the Germans had been right – she was insatiable. If he'd stayed much longer she would have crippled him and he'd have been late for sailing. The mate, dreaming as usual of a liberated Spain, had been flaked out in the saloon; the ship would never have been ready if he, the captain, Gonzales Zapiola, had not roused out the crew from the café on the quay.

He blinked and shook his head to clear the alcoholic fumes. This fog was the devil . . . if he missed Cap Gris Nez, he was bound to pick up ZC 2 or the wreck buoy. It was suddenly colder out here – the clamminess was eating through his bones. He pulled down the brim of his Panama hat, flicked the dark glasses further across the bridge of his nose and retreated into the wheelhouse where he lit up a Havana. He watched the circles of smoke swirling across the comforting fug of the boxed-in bridge.

He glanced at his reflection in one of the windows: the puffiness beneath his bloodshot eyes was exaggerating his age – he had packed more experience into his thirty-eight years than men twice his age. The paunch hanging over his belted tropical trousers was something of which he was proud – Gonzales Zapiola was enjoying his new way of life. When honest with himself, he admitted that he had been lucky to land this job. Though he had been slung out from the naval academy, he had done well later as a conscript during his training in the *Liberdad*.

His ability in the rigging had much to do with his relative success. Armed with a good testimonial, he had begun the circuit as a junior officer in the Argentinian Merchant Marine. He had managed to scrape his Second Mate's ticket whilst on the meat run to the European ports, but he had grown sick of the boredom. Two years in the Mediterranean followed, in Cypriot and Liberian coasters, running general cargoes. Then, last year, he had seen the notice in the agent's office in the Piraeus . . .

'*Capitano* . . . there's a hooter close to starboard.' Adolfo was calling from the starboard wing, through the half-opened door.

The melancholy siren from Cap Gris Nez sounded too near. He flicked the auto-pilot to port: he'd bring her round for a few minutes. He would pick up zc 2 buoy any moment – his luck usually held when he was buoy hopping: the Channel was well provided with marks, even though the buoyage this side of the Channel was different from that on the British side. He couldn't be expected to understand the numerous differing systems.

The agent for his Greek owners had accepted without a qualm his limited qualifications: he had been forced to wait a few days for the Master's certificate, but they had had the nerve to deduct the cost of its procurement from his first month's pay . . . bloody rogues. Since then, he had been master of his ship and he carried out orders without a murmur. After running arms into the Lebanon for a few months, they had sent for him and landed him with this latest assignment.

On his first run through the Strait of Dover to Hamburg, the weather had been perfect: hot sun, unlimited visibility, flat calm. The sealed containers, entered in the bill of loading as 'Agricultural Fertilizer', had been stowed in the bottom of the holds by the night shifts, whilst he and his crew had savoured the delights of the German port. His orders were to return to Boulogne and pick up the scrap metal which was to be loaded above the Hamburg cargo. He was then to proceed to Middlesborough on the east coast of England (he had the devil of a job finding a chart of the area) where he was to discharge the scrap. He was then to proceed ostensibly to Glasgow, north-about. Once clear of the Orkneys, he was to remain outside the Hebrides and steam south-south-west into the Atlantic, keeping two hundred miles to the westward of Ireland. When in latitude 50° north (they weren't fussy about accuracy and he had assured them that his DR navigation was accurate enough) he was to dump the rest of the cargo into the Atlantic. They were doubling the crew's monthly pay and were handing him five thousand dollars, half now, and half on completion of the job. The Hamburg agent had said nothing – merely handed the cash across the desk.

He brought *Castello* back to starboard ... he had forgotten how long he had been on this course, but he would turn up and hope to find the next buoy if he had missed the last two. It was already 1609 ... they must be astern by now, and neither could he hear the siren from Cap Gris Nez. He had heard one ship's fog-horn, somewhere on his port beam. The sound had stayed with him for some time, passing up his port side. He might be closer to the north-east bound lane than he thought. He would bring her back to the eastward again for a bit, to clear out of the way ... It was lucky he was a born seaman; he reckoned he could smell danger when it threatened, but he had better try to make some sense out of all the navigational warnings, chart corrections, port regulations, sailing directions, channel routing instructions – God, what mountains of paperwork! He tipped on to the chart-table a heap of official mail, booklets and paper that the agent had dumped on him in Hamburg.

'Shout if you see anything, Adolfo ...'

Castello's engines pounded away, a comforting accompaniment in this frightening fog. He would ease down if he did not find the buoys soon, but he could not afford to be late at Middlesbrough. The owners had also seen to that: for every six hours he was adrift on an ETA, they were docking a day's pay. Crafty bastards ... with *Castello de Sierra* wearing her Liberian flag, though she was Portugese-built, registered in the Piraeus, administered by a Greek limited company and crewed by a Latin-American-Spanish crew, there was little that international officialdom could do ... He smiled contentedly to himself, his thick lips licking round the fat cigar. He extracted the new chart of the Dover Strait which the agent had insisted on giving him.

Gonzales's limited English allowed him to decipher the meaning of the traffic separation zones – they were plain enough. But, as for

the navigational warnings of the buoys off-station and all the rest
... he suddenly scooped up the heap of paper and stuffed it
violently into the drawer. There was one aid he liked and which
was fitted in *Castello* – the MF radio direction finder.

Why weren't ships beamed up channel and into ports, as the
aircraft were? And why, for pity's sake, didn't the charts tell you
what to do, clearly and precisely, when someone like him was
approaching a congested channel or entering a port for the first
time? Why couldn't he be told on the chart what beacons he had
to keep ahead, what bearings to run down – and what radio
frequency to guard? He cursed and switched the receiver to 2182,
the distress wave. He would leave the set on now that he was
approaching the worst traffic, but, apart from emergencies, 2182
was useless ...

Gonzales was pouring over the chart, deciding where to cross
the lanes, when he almost rammed the wreck buoy to the west of
Calais. His attention had been distracted by the radio which was
crackling behind him: some stupid yacht, English by the sound of
it, was monopolizing the frequency: 'North Foreland, North
Foreland, this is motor yacht, *Doreen Rose, Doreen Rose* ... How
d'yer read me?' Irritably, Zapiola turned down the volume.

Castello was suddenly moving about ... uncomfortable motion
... he could hear waves slapping against her sides. He moved out
to the port wing, and true enough, she was passing through
confused water. He returned to the chart, as Adolfo pushed his
head excitedly through the door: 'Black and red buoy to starboard, *Capitano*.'

Captain Zapiola's fat finger stabbed at the chart: he must be in
the outfalls off the Calais wreck buoy. He would turn to the northward now, as the Boulogne trawler skipper had advised him. He
would cross the shipping lanes for South Falls and the North Sea
by passing close north of the separation zone and Sandettié lightvessel. He wished he could know what was coming down from
the north-east, and up from the south-west astern of him. It was
no use trying 2182 – and his tight-fisted owners had refused him
VHF, so he could not use Channel 16. They had told him at
Boulogne to watch out for the Dover Coastguard which tracked

all ships passing through the Straits. Anyone breaking the new routing rules was reported to officialdom. But the Coastguard also provided a service and reported each half hour all shipping movements passing through the Straits. He could have made use of the service at this minute – but they used Channel 10 which was bugger all use to a small ship like *Castello de Sierra*.

'Take the wheel, Adolfo,' he yelled through the door. 'Bring her round to 005°. I'm crossing the lanes now.'

He moved to the chart table and pencilled a cross beside the wreck buoy; then, unusually for him, he recorded the time of his estimated position – 1640.

He went outside. He screwed up his eyes as he glared into the yellow blanket swirling about the ship. He did not relish charging blindly through this stuff, but he would keep her at full speed to get across the lanes as rapidly as he could.

From somewhere on his port hand he thought he heard a foghorn. For the first time, he felt anxious. He moved quickly to the fog lanyard and tugged. *Castello*'s horn vibrated feebly, coughed, spluttered, then died. Gonzales swore . . . better perhaps this way. No one would notice him and, even if he was picked up on radar by the Dover people, they certainly would be unable to identify him.

'Course, *Capitano*, 005°,' Adolfo reported.

Zapiola grunted and sucked at his cigar. In an hour's time he would be in the worst bit – just west of Sandettié lightship.

CHAPTER 7

Motor Yacht
Doreen Rose IV

'How do I look, Ron?' Barbara Cooper called up through the saloon door. 'D'you like your mate, Captain Bligh?'

She could hear him pottering about on the high bridge above her head. He always became difficult just before sailing, his mind elsewhere, other then where she liked it to be. He was too enthralled today with his new radar toy to take much interest in her – and after she had bought this smashing outfit for him, too. She prinked up her curls again, then knotted the anchor-motif scarf carefully about her head. Her hair-do would have to be sacrificed – too bad, but she could have another set in that fabulous 'coiffeuse' in Blankenberge, if *Doreen Rose* cleared the Belgian customs before the shops shut. She drooped against the doorway, as she heard him descending the ladder.

'D'you call, luv?'

His eyes fell to her low-necked jumper as he entered the saloon. She wore no bra, for he liked her this way. She moved towards him, coaxing him to the settee.

'When we get over to the other side, Babs,' he said. 'With this fog, we don't know how long the trip'll take.' He smacked her bottom and crossed to the drawer for his binoculars.

Mr Ronald Tykely was okay. Barbara enjoyed her relationship with him as his private assistant. Not yet forty, he had fought his way to the top and was now managing director of Sheppey Motors (Sales and Service) Limited, the largest used car dealers in East Kent. With the cash that he handled, there was always something doing – there was never a dull day with Mr Tykely.

As she watched him fumbling in one of the lockers, she realized that she was growing attached to this very basic man.

He was a small, podgy mini-tycoon, and a veritable dynamo. If he could put as much energy into his work as he exercised elsewhere, the company would be doing better. His trouble was that too many funds were side-tracked into fiddles like *Doreen Rose IV*. His paunch already drooped over his belt, but he still had that powerful animal look about him which she enjoyed. He looked good in that captain's cap with the frilly gold braid, which he always squashed on to his balding head as soon as he picked her up in the Jag. The L-shaped sideboards which smothered his face were in keeping with the jolly-tar image, but she wondered how much he sported the affectation to hide the blotchy pink unhealthiness that too much drinking caused . . . she smiled back at him, as his piggy eyes turned on her.

'Coming uptop?' he asked. 'We're ready for the "off".' He slung the binoculars around his neck, caressed her vaguely as he pushed his way past her, and hurried up the ladder.

'I'm useless as a sailor,' she yelled after him. 'I've taken my pills.'

'Come up and decorate the joint. You can sit on the sun deck.'

'Bloody hell,' she swore softly to herself. 'What's he take me for?' – but she carefully hauled herself up to the enclosed lounge where she could watch, yet still be sheltered from the wind. She collected a couple of cushions and settled herself down to watch the fun. Something always went wrong when he left the harbour. Ramsgate with its lock and high moles was not easy, she supposed, but there were hilarious moments when Captain Tykely tried to take his *Doreen Rose IV* to sea . . . she watched him as he went to the back to let go the ropes.

Poor old Ron – if only he knew how the world smiled at him behind his back . . . Did he really think that his wife did not realize what was going on? Perhaps by now she did not care . . . Doreen, she was; Rose, the obnoxious daughter, fourteen years old, yet fast enough to pass for a Southend tart . . . The boat bumped suddenly up in the front – Ron rushed past her and scrambled up the prow-bridge towering above. There was a shout, then she heard the starters whirring and the engines bursting into life. She felt for her cigarettes and lit up. Thank God they were off . . . Only a couple of hours of hell and she could feel dry land beneath her feet again. It was twenty-four minutes past four as the lighthouse on the end of the mole slid past high above her.

Ron Tykely was glad to be at sea again, even though this fog was bloody . . . but he'd had so much of it during the past fortnight that he was almost growing used to it. And the new radar, which he had entered up in the Miscellaneous column as Motorsport Equipment, would transform the situation. What better way of becoming handy with the gadget than having to use it seriously on his way across to Zeebrugge – or Ostend, if he missed the first?

He would make for the North Goodwin lightship; he would look out for the Channel buoys at the north end of the Gull and the Goodwin Knoll, and would keep a bit to the northward to pick up the lightship. From North Goodwin he could feel his way down on radar to the East Goodwin lightship. He could put *Doreen* on 'George' whilst he played with the radar on his way down . . . he glanced up with pleasure at the enclosed scanner which was whirring away satisfactorily inside its plastic dome. Smart bit of work that . . . he knocked twenty per cent off the listed price.

He had not bothered to ring up the coastguard. He never worried them – they had enough on their plate these days. His ETD never bore much relation to the truth and he'd be lucky today to make an accurate ETA. He would make Zeebrugge if he could, because the Belgians, keen to do reciprocal business, were waiting to give him a slap-up dinner in Bruges. He hadn't told them about Babs – she'd be furious if she wasn't invited along too . . . He pushed the twin throttles forwards and worked *Doreen Rose* up to three-quarter speed, 2300 revs which gave her twenty-four knots; he could hear North Goodwin's diaphone booming well on his starboard quarter. He had not sighted the buoys which must now be well clear.

There was the lightship . . . he took the boat gently round to the southward and put 'George' on 175° magnetic. He could act like a big ship and take the best channel down to East Goodwin, instead of crossing the Falls – he didn't like the seas there. He glanced at the chart: Goodwin buoys all had reflectors. He'd pick them up and that would take him well clear of the Sands. He had forgotten to look at the tides, but he knew it was about high tide, so there'd be slack water off the Goodwins. It was good to feel the power beneath his feet – he felt the thrill, as he always did when once he was on his way, of being master of his own craft.

He tucked himself into the visor . . . what a bloody foul-up – nothing but bright traces all round. The strobe was only just visible and he might as well be in the middle of the Sahara. He began fumbling with the knobs, but it was no use; he must find the instruction manual.

By the time he had read the first page again, he had forgotten where he was. The drone of the engines and the slap-slap of the water against the hard chines had a soporific effect . . . he had better be more alert or he'd hit something. He poked his head above the windshield. He gasped as the moisture-filled air hit his lungs.

1646 . . . he must be coming up to the north-east Goodwin buoy by now. Damn, he had forgotten to log the time at the lightship – must have been about five past five. He dived back to his radar.

By the time he had some sort of picture on his screen, the time had slipped round to 1702 – and as he peered again through the fog he felt the first twinge of panic. No sign of the East Goodwin buoy either – and he could not be far from the wreck on the sands which showed even at high water. The PPI seemed a mass of echoes, and suddenly he was confused and disorientated by this unfamiliar world. He had better knock down the revs, or he'd rip the bottom out of her if he touched . . .

'What's happening, Ron?'

Babs's high-pitched voice irritated him at this moment. He'd be having hysterics on his hands next. 'Nothing to worry about, luv. Looking for the East Goodwin lightship. Help yourself to the Scotch – and you can hand me up one too.' She disappeared back to the sunlounge deck.

The chuckle of the exhausts pleased him, as he took the boat round in a wide sweep to port. If he could not sight something soon, he was buggered ... it was more difficult to return to Ramsgate now than to feel his way across – if it wasn't for the shipping lanes. He was considering asking the coastguard for a position, when there was a shriek from aft.

'Ron, watch out ... you nearly hit it.' The woman was angry, damn her eyes.

'What's up?'

'That buoy ... didn't you see it?' She was pointing out to port.

'Course not ... d'you read its name?'

'South-east something ... Couldn't catch the rest.'

'What colour?'

'Sort of rusty-red.'

He slammed the engines to stop and pulled the chart up to his seat ... there, SE Goodwins buoy. Before he could forget, he scribbled the time beside it: 1714. As he did so, he heard the mournful wail of the lightship's diaphone just astern.

'Okay, Babs. I know where we are. Where's me Scotch?'

He would feel his way across to the East Goodwin lightship. Once there, he'd make for the South Falls buoy. Then he would cut across the lane to the Sandettié north-west buoy. Even if *Doreen*'s plastic hull did not provide too good an echo to other ships, she had a turn of speed and could look after herself. He was beginning to understand the radar, so what the hell ... He pushed up the revs again and began singing to himself as he felt her gathering speed.

CHAPTER 8

Hoverferry
Watson Watt

Thursday, 3 June
Wind: Force 2, ENE
Visibility: 100 yards

Terence Kemp was twenty-six years old, ex-Clan Line and a product of the Warsash Navigational School. He was sitting in the window seat of a British Rail second-class smoker and staring with distaste at the fog sweeping across the cliff, while the train rattled its last few miles from Folkestone to Dover.

In spite of his morning off (one forenoon a week), Kemp was an unhappy man this afternoon: first, he had been up half the night suffering from the effects of stale prawns which he had eaten in the pub to which Susan and he had been invited by his opposite number, the navigator of the other hoverferry, *Sir Alec Rose*; and second, Kemp was not looking forward to meeting his captain, after yesterday's débâcle.

The train emerged from the cutting and tore along the sea's edge preceding the run-in to Dover Priory. The Channel was a bright silver-grey that hurt the eyes with its glare. The shingle beach flashed past and the sea, merging into the formless horizon, looked brown and uninviting. Visibility had shut right down, probably two hundred yards at the most. This would be a hard day, having to stare incessantly into his radar screen. Thank God he had taken the job as *Watson Watt*'s navigating officer for the summer months only . . . but somehow he had to survive today and try to regain Captain Jones's confidence. If he failed, he would

48

be out on his ear, and Susan, his adorable wife of three months standing, would not think much of a failed hoverferry officer. It was good to arrive home at their Folkestone flat at the end of a day's work – his watch covered one trip in the forenoon and two in the second half of the day.

The train was slowing down – he wondered whether Douglas Townsend would be waiting to give him the customary lift to the hoverport this afternoon. As chief officer of hoverferry *Watson Watt*, Townsend's first loyalty was to Captain Aloysius Jones.

Terence Kemp yesterday had wrongly identified a buoy. Travelling through fog at speed demanded perfect liaison between navigator and captain. In communication only by headset (the noise of the pounding hovercraft made ordinary conversation impossible) the captain interpreted the radar picture solely by the voice of his navigator.

It was not the wrong identification which had been so disastrous: the unforgiveable sin was Kemp's attempt to cover up his mistake. This deception had destroyed the intangible trust which was vital between captain and navigator. Terence had panicked and felt terrible about his failure, particularly as the incident was now common knowledge amongst his brother officers.

Watson Watt's bridge team consisted of Captain Aloysius, thirty-four, a quick-tempered Welshman who did not suffer fools gladly; the chief officer and second-in-command, Douglas Townsend, also thirty-four – and Terence Kemp. Both Jones and Townsend had their Master's tickets and ten years bridge experience in the Merchant Service. Kemp possessed his First Mate's certificate and had been at sea for eight years. Normally *Watson Watt*'s officers were a relaxed and efficient team: neither ship nor aircraft, the hovercraft service had developed its own techniques.

Townsend was waiting in his Capri outside the station.

'Afternoon, Terry. Nearly couldn't make it: had to take the kids to the dentist.' Townsend lived in Dover, preferring it to Ramsgate where accommodation was impossible. During the drive to the new hoverport, which Hoverferries had built in the north corner of Pegwell Bay, neither man referred to yesterday's incident. On arrival, each went his separate way, Townsend to the briefing room, Kemp to the office to pick up the most recent navigational warnings. In twenty minutes *Watson Watt* was due.

The change-over between crews was a routine affair, never taking more than a few minutes. By the time the new crew had carried out its pre-flight checks, the cars would have been stowed on the car deck and the passengers safely ensconced in their seats. Most of the traffic during these hot weeks consisted of British day-visitors to France.

Watson Watt, a Mark II hoverferry, was performing well after her minor teething troubles. She had been running without a break for nine weeks, but was not making her speed because the skirt was showing signs of wear. But, with fifty-two knots, her performance was ample for her schedules, in spite of the fogs bedevilling the Straits at this time of year.

Kemp forced himself towards the small gathering of officers waiting outside the Mess for the craft to emerge from the fog. It was all routine, but in this stuff, Terry felt nervous – so much of the load depended on his rapid assessments – and his nausea did not help this morning. He was not looking forward to being cooped up in that heaving black box and crouched over the PPI for twenty-five minutes. He could not go sick today, if he wanted to keep his job.

Thank God, it was almost impossible to have an emergency in these craft. With fifty-plus knots under her kilt, the ships were treated as stopped targets and the hovercraft steered for the hole. With nil visibility, the Mark I Eyeball method was useless: there was a 'dead' distance ahead of the bow for at least 300 yards – and this was when the innumerable yachts became a menace ... Terence disliked them more than all other targets, because he never knew what they would do next.

'Afternoon, sir.'

The captain, in his epauletted white shirt and with hands on his hips, did not return the salute. He nodded and turned his head, his suspicious eyes momentarily meeting Terry's. 'There's a lot about today, Kemp. I'll maintain normal speed, so long as you keep me accurately informed. Any new notices?'

'There's the new landfall buoy, sir, two miles south-east of Sandettié south-west buoy.'

Through the fog they could hear the roar of the approaching hovercraft. They stared down the shrouded concrete ramp, towards the wet sand shimmering in the heat of this hot June afternoon. From out of the glare the grotesque shape of *Watson Watt* appeared like a spectre. She approached the ramp between the buoyed approach path leading up into this northern corner of Pegwell Bay where the second hoverport had been built. As the machine bore down on them, the pitch of the propellers changed: the engines revolved on the axes of their pedestals and the hoverferry floated crabwise towards them. At the last moment, she swivelled, cut her engines and deflated. Another trip was over.

The unloading ramps opened across the stern and, as the first cars began rolling from the car deck, Kemp followed Captain Jones up the ladder and into the cockpit to take over from the departing watch. Terry dived into the seclusion of his navigational cabinet, a miniscule and centrally screened section in the centre and behind the captain's and chief officer's seats. Trying to ignore the nausea, he prepared for the next run across to Hoverferry's new hoverport which had been built to the east of Calais.

The captain and chief officer were already carrying out their pre-flight checks: jet-pipe temperatures, torque, prop control pressures . . . so often they had exercised the drill but, as always, the checks had to be systematic and meticulously carried out. Terry scrutinized his radars and tested communications on Channels 1 and 2. He heard the engines running up, then the hooter as the skirt inflated . . . they were off, right on time: 1720.

The craft bucked as she turned. She crabbed her way across the ramp, then slid to the sand as the Old Man switched on the water jets of his windscreen wipers to clear the spume. Another half an hour and it would be high water – they could safely cross the Goodwins.

The black conical buoy slid past their starboard side, as the captain increased the pitch: twenty . . . thirty knots. The craft swung down the buoyed lane and Terry Kemp felt the slap as the hoverferry hit the sea. He screwed his head into the visor: his screen was speckled with echoes, as he began chanting ranges and bearings to the captain. He swallowed the bile that rose in his gorge and tried to forget his nausea.

'There's a concentration of echoes off Sandettié, sir,' he reported.

'Roger,' Captain Jones snapped. 'Give me the hole and I'll go for it.'

The roar of the engines drowned all else as *Watson Watt* charged through the fog for the Goodwins at fifty-two knots.

The owner of the old Dormobile, registration number BUO 714, lay back in the comfortable seat, his wife by his side. He was exhausted by all the last minute rush – green cards, tickets, shutting up the house – and was thankful to have a few minutes rest before reaching Calais. He and Gladys had been saving up the whole year for this week's adventure. Her brother had lent them the old van and Glad had filled up every corner with tins of food which were so expensive on the continent.

He, too, had stocked up: he had taken on loan a set of engine spares and bought cans of oil. He had even scrounged two old Jerry cans from the works. They were ex-wartime and the rubber seals on the filler caps had perished. He had cut out some replacements from an old inner tube, though one cap fitted better than the other. So, having tanked up outside Ramsgate, he was topped right up and saving quite a bit on petrol – the foreign stuff was still more expensive.

They had told him on the car deck to leave the van in gear, but they knew nothing of her dicky gear-box. She'd be all right as he had left her, with the hand brake on as hard as he dared. The huge car deck was crammed to capacity: he had counted thirty-three other cars. He had tried to be last on, so that he could be first off (they unloaded over the ramp at the back end) but they had shoved him in the middle. There was a big Princess on one side of him, but even if the van moved about, it couldn't do much damage with those big Honda bikes stacked up on the other side.

The tired man glanced at his watch: twenty-four minutes past five. They were due at Calais at 1735 British time . . . he closed his eyes and let the incessant pounding of the hoverferry lull him to sleep.

CHAPTER 9

Dover Straits Coastguard

1727, Thursday, 3 June
Wind on clifftop, Operations Centre, St Margaret's Bay:
Force 2, ENE
Visibility: Nil

Coastguard John Tranter stood for a moment at the bottom of the steps leading up to the operations room of the Coastguard Rescue Headquarters which was perched on the cliff 300 feet above the sea. Wads of yellow fog were curling across the lip of the precipice, unpleasant thick stuff from the Downs and the Goodwins, those shifting and treacherous sand banks which lay four miles from the foot of St Margaret's cliff. The fog was patchy and, through gaps in the blanket, Tranter caught glimpses of the rock-pools extending from the beach into the swirling tideway.

He enjoyed these rare breaks. At fifty-five he was the oldest of the team and it was difficult sometimes to contain the memories that obtruded upon the realities of the present. How could a man in his thirties understand the emotions of the older generation when, to the day nearly forty years ago, these same waters were covered to the horizon by the Little Ship Armada streaming across from Dunkirk?

Before joining submarines, Tranter had been a boy-seaman in *Malcolm*, one of the last destroyers to slip from Dunkirk's shell-pierced jetties. After the evacuation, when Britain had made ready for action, the coastal convoys began fighting their way through the Downs, easterly and westerly, twice a week, from the Thames to Portsmouth.

The shelling from the German guns began at Ramsgate; the 'time of flight' interval was seventy-five seconds from gun-flash on Cap Gris Nez to shell-splash at the Downs. Even now he could see it all – the flickering fire from the French coast, the long wait, then the whistle-blast from the bridge which caused so much amusement, but which was the signal for all hands on the upper deck to prostrate themselves; the flash and the crack as the shells exploded – then the long, rolling boom of the original gunfire reverberating from the southern horizon.

When the convoy was plodding against the tide, the ordeal lasted five hours, until the little ships reached the south-west Folkestone buoy where the shelling suddenly ceased.

That was long ago, but up here on the cliff-top, identical flowers still nodded their heads, the same grasses still bent to the breeze. The thyme must have been the same, a purple patchwork across the cliffhead, sweetly scented, delicious on the air; at his feet, wheeling below the cliff-top, the gulls still cried their warnings to the choughs flapping lazily against the background of the chalky precipice.

Tranter pulled himself together, dragged at the last of his cigarette. The fog rolled away to the westward: a Victorian villa showed briefly; then, on the cliff edge, loomed the massive outline of Dover castle, two and a half miles away. Behind him, the apex of the Dover Patrol obelisk was shrouded in mist. Two generations were remembered here: the dead of the Kaiser's war; and, on another plaque at the foot of the memorial, those who perished in these waters nearly forty years ago . . . how futile it all seemed now. He gazed to the northward where Ramsgate and Pegwell Bay lazed in the sunlight where the fog had dispersed.

The fog was closing in again. These Straits bore a different menace now: millions of tons of oil were transported daily through these restricted seas. At any moment, day or night, this incomparable shore line could be desecrated for years. And he, in his miniscule way, was one of the first enlisted pioneers trying to do something to avert the inevitable disaster. He climbed the steps slowly, the crescent giant scanner of the radar whirring above him on the roof of the Centre.

Inside the operations room, the watch was quietly going about its business: the senior watch officer was putting the final touches to Part One of the Information Bulletin about to be broadcast on Channel 10. The last of the weather and visibility reports from the lightvessels were being sifted; the reports from the ships which had voluntarily registered their positions were being assessed to complete the broad picture; several vessels, two of them drawing over sixty feet, had reported that they could not comply with the separation scheme because of the fog and their inability to man-oeuvre – and one VLCC had been forced to anchor in the separation zone three miles east of the Varne. These were the good boys and naturally would not be reported to their governments as rogues.

Tranter manned his post at the left-hand end of the long window overlooking the invisible Channel. The Surveillance Station at Cap Gris Nez, manned by French national servicemen, was at this moment confirming with St Margaret's Bay its agree-ment for the next broadcast. Only nineteen miles distant and visible as soon as the fog cleared, the French were attacking this business with Gallic logic. Already, they were legislating for all French ships to listen to the Surveillance broadcasts and to maintain continuous radio guard on Channel 11 when passing through the Pas de Calais.

'Anything else for *General Information*, John?' the watch officer was asking. 'I've got seventeen ships so far and one rogue crossing from Boulogne for *Traffic Information*. Any one else?'

The Senior Watch Officer's skill lay in producing a simple and accurate report: too much or irrelevant information irritated over-stressed masters. One experienced captain had remarked: 'I don't often listen to Dover Straits Coastguard: it's too depressing,' but another had written: 'Thanks to you, I can now sleep at night.'

'Yes, sir. There's something coming down from the North Goodwin. It's a weak echo and off the south-east Goodwin buoy; seems to be making across for the lightvessel – speed about twenty knots. Probable power-boat pleasure-craft . . .'

The watch officer nodded to the auxiliary coastguard in the corner, Pamela Wainwright.

'Stand-by the 1740 broadcast,' he ordered. Then he turned to Tranter.

'John, get hold of the Inspector on his bleeper. A dangerous situation is developing.'

Outside, the diaphone from the South Goodwin lightvessel grunted through the mists. Then, seconds later, the low resonant boom of a fog-horn sounded. Somewhere in that shrouded world, a giant VLCC was feeling its way through the congested Straits.

CHAPTER 10

Harbour Master, East Thames

1725, Thursday, 3 June
Wind: Force 3, SSE
Visibility: 6 miles

'Sorry, sir. We still haven't received *Bir-Hakeim*'s ETA.'

Captain Gratton nodded, then rubbed the stubble on his chin as he concentrated on tomorrow's movements. Irritating – Universal's Berthing Superintendent had applied enough pressure to get her into the head of tomorrow's queue, but she still had not come up with a firm ETA, nor asked for clearance inwards. Though the remainder of the other movements were wrapped up, they depended on *Bir-Hakeim* because of the tug situation.

'Let's try St Margaret's Bay. Get me the inspector on the phone.'

Gratton had had enough today. He would quit as soon as he was happy about tomorrow's movements, but he could not do so until he had something firm on *Bir-Hakeim*.

All this uncertainty could be avoided if only some order could be imposed on the shipping fraternity. Entrance to the Thames estuary began well beyond the Straits now: if a ship demanded a guaranteed berth, she had to signal her intentions in plenty of time. If she failed to comply with the PLA's directions a powerful persuader was the sanction of a ship missing her berth, because the available deep-draught anchorages were scarce. There was a point of no return in most of these deep movements. In the Thames now all ships had to comply with a form of mandatory routing and zonal control. How else could the river be organized?

'Dover Straits Coastguard on the line, sir.'

'Senior Watch Officer here. Sorry, sir, but Captain Tuson is with the D of T at Langdon Bay, checking the plans for the new centre.'

'I wanted a word with him about Universal's lightener, *Bir-Hakeim*. Can you give me her position?' In the background, Gratton could hear the murmur of R/T procedure, the ringing of telephones.

'We're very pushed at the moment, sir. Could you wait a few minutes?'

'Of course. I'll ring back.'

Stuart Gratton replaced his phone. Patience was not his strong point. He would contact his son, Bill, while his staff were working through *Bir-Hakeim*'s planned passage diagram. Universal had confirmed that she was at her maximum loaded draught of forty-eight feet, so that she would need all the water she could find.

All depended on whether she could be off Longsand Head on time: it was fifty miles up to the oil havens from the Trinity buoy. The planned passage ensured her safe run over the shoal water, provided she complied with the ordered speeds. A ship drawing up to forty-eight feet could safely be navigated up to the oil port on spring tides by using the flood to lift her across the shallow patches. Provided she entered the Black Deep at the earliest opportunity and reported at the Way Points, his team in the control room at Gravesend could adjust her speed on the way up to ensure a good arrival.

The amount of water under her keel was what mattered: these big ships, if steaming too fast in shallow water, 'squatted', thereby effectively increasing their draught. The procedure was somewhat like Victor Sylvester's 'slow-quick-quick-slow' rhythm: too fast, and she would run out of water on the way; too slow, and she would be too late for arrival at high water off her berth. Both varieties had figured in his experiences over the years.

Gratton always felt at home here in the Control Centre of the Thames Navigation Service at Gravesend. It was, after all, his own dream-child and he had been with it since its conception. The crescent-shaped room was the closest resemblance to a bridge console that he was likely to see from now on. The watch consisted of a master mariner in supervisory charge and three radio officers complete with all their modern communications – VHF radio telephones and shore-line connections to the pilots, tugs, quarantine and dock officials, as well as telex to the world and radio links from the chain of tide guages.

The entire passage from the outer limits to London, including the Way Points where the ships were required to report their passing, was displayed on the perspex plot on the opposite wall. Below each section, a corresponding radar displayed the traffic picture to the duty officer. All went well so long as masters, pilots and owners played ball.

In the early days, problems had arisen when ships had jumped the queue and nudged their way up the channels as of old. But the advent of specialized and hazardous cargoes had changed all that . . . The powers of 'Special Direction' now authorized the Harbour Master to regulate the movements of ships, especially those with such cargoes, for the benefit of the common good.

He caught the eye of the duty officer. 'Would you try a link call to *Niger Petrola* for me, please? I'll take it in my office.'

To cool his heels, he would remain here, observing the run of traffic. There were still too many unresolved problems, the most difficult being indemnity in case of accident. The ship-master was now required to obey the authority's orders, so long as he did not see these as imperilling his ship's safety; but if these instructions caused an accident or expensive delays, who was liable? The insurance companies had resolved their problem for multiple pile-ups in fog on the motorways . . . Britain's Port Authorities could not expect luck on their side for ever.

'You're second turn, sir. North Foreland have heard *Niger* – about five minutes.'

Stuart Gratton nodded. The Authority was lucky to have held together a good team, but with the present traffic explosion, how was high quality personnel to be recruited in the future? Good men cost money. These Control Centres needed men who were combined master mariners, port managers and good communicators – an expensive blend. Outside guilds and individuals could

59

not satisfy these requirements. But surely, with the importance which society rightly attached to the protection of the environment, government must help pay for the training of the personnel and the provision of the equipment?

Our ports were generally sited on river estuaries and would soon be compelled to provide marine traffic systems. The approach channels were often narrow and shallow, needing costly dredging for today's deep-draught ships. Although society and the ports generally were seeing the need to control the conduct of ships in these waters, it was taking years to convince the shipping industry and the institutions that most of the law under which they conducted their affairs belonged to the days of sail. The new-found 'powers of direction' were a triumph in their way – the first of an era. His team had pioneered all that – right here in London.

Though the safety record of our marine pilots (the shipmasters' advisers) was unsurpassed, accidents still occurred because of the lack of standardized procedures – the hidden costs to harbours and to the shipping industry, owing to accidents and to delays, was astronomical. One serious accident could cost more to the environment and to society than all the money needed to set up a national, standard port control system.

'Your call, sir.'

He slipped through to his office, closing the door behind him. The phone clicked and *Niger Petrola*'s radio officer was talking at the other end.

'Just a minute, sir. I'll get the captain.'

A fog-horn blared in the background. Bill came on.

'Hi, Dad. You okay?'

'Fine, and so's your mother. You bound for Fredericia?'

'Saturday afternoon. I'll ring you in the evening.' He added: 'How're Prue and the kids?'

'All well, Bill. Looking forward to seeing you. Any chance of your touching England?'

'Must ring off. Sorry, Dad. It's bloody thick here. I'm running up to the Sandettié. Take care, Dad.'

The phone clicked, then North Foreland chipped in.

'Three minutes, sir.'

Stuart Gratton set down the phone. He was continually moaning about the need for the adoption of standard Area Procedures to make easier the life of globe-trotting masters and ships, in addition to aiding those helping them ashore. But he would not relish Bill's task at this moment: navigating a VLCC through the Straits in thick fog needed a special sort of courage, a unique breed of man.

He hauled himself from his chair and reached for his jacket. It was 1727 and time to pack up. The fog was already shutting down in the lower reaches; it would be cold on his way home to Rochester.

PART TWO

CHAPTER II

Motor Yacht
Doreen Rose IV

1722, Thursday, 3 June
Wind: Force 2, ENE
Visibility: 50 yards

The roar of the engines and the whine of the superchargers gave Ron Tykely the reassurance he needed, as *Doreen Rose* ploughed towards the South Falls buoy. She was maintaining her twenty-four knots, 'George' had steadied her nicely on course, and he had mastered the brilliance control on his radar. He sighed with relief as the blip of the buoy came up broad on his port bow. A couple of minutes and it would be abeam, half-a-mile to port – excellent. He was on the long range scale; he had not yet discerned how to switch to scale one and would try in a moment.

There were too many other echoes on the screen to bother about all of them: something was well clear and slipping down his port quarter from the South Falls. Two big fellows were coming up the north-east lane; they were astern on his starboard quarter and just ahead of a smaller blip crossing to the northward.

He was not sure about the two large echoes bearing down upon him in his south-west lane. They were fine on his port bow but seemed close on this scale: one, the more northern of the two, was the closer – she must be the more dangerous. He would cross ahead of her and come to starboard if he had to . . . he slithered to the chart table and ran his rule up to the north Sandettié buoy . . . 070° magnetic from the South Falls which was coming up . . . He leaned across and set 'George' 15° to port. The boat swayed, listed, then steadied to her new course. He was pencilling in the time, 1722, when he felt Bab's arm encircling his waist.

'Hi, sweetie . . . it's lonely down there.'

He could smell the drink. He pushed her to the outboard edge of the seat.

'I'm busy, Babs. If you want to make yourself useful, get me another Scotch.'

The excitement of these channel crossings provided the exhilaration he missed in his humdrum business life. It was all go out here – there was no one to whom he could pass the buck. One cock-up in this fog, and his insurance broker wouldn't be making his holiday to the Costa Brava this year. What the hell was the matter with Babs? She could sulk if she wanted; there was a time and place, dammit.

'Hey, where's my Scotch?'

He poked his head back into the radar visor. He would fiddle with the scale control and see if he could not produce a more realistic picture . . . first, the manual. The trouble with power boats was the bloody noise they made – couldn't hear anything else while the engines were running. Ah, here it was . . . three scales . . . he'd been switching the wrong way. He fumbled with the knob, twisted and felt the click as it engaged.

The screen faded and the new picture emerged – three wide concentric circles instead of the half-dozen, closely spaced: one-and-a-half mile scale, the handbook said. He had better remove his digit – five minutes had slipped by: 1727 already.

Christ, what was that? A bloody great echo – dead ahead and *inside* the inner circle . . . and then he heard the boom of a fog-horn very close. His head shot from the visor. The invisible ship was directly ahead and running him down . . . he flicked the auto-pilot to 'hand' and grabbed the wheel. As he wrenched her off to starboard to cross the track of the approaching menace, Babs screamed.

She was pointing upwards, over the starboard bow. Her mouth was slack and the glass she was holding fell to the deck. The yellow fog grew suddenly more dense, deeper, darker . . . He felt the kick in his guts as he recognized the peril. He spun the wheel,

66

hard-a-port . . . his only chance to clear out of it before the bulbous bow rolled them under.

Doreen Rose IV heeled hard to port. A white mountain lunged from out of the haze. The water boiled and heaved; suddenly the motor boat was pounding down the side of the monstrous, white ship's side disappearing into the fog above them.

The ship's starboard quarter caught the top of the boot-topping. Ron saw the paint flying, felt *Doreen* list back to starboard as she buried her bows. Instinctively, he flung the port engine control to 'stop', then went full astern. She shuddered from the violent torque, then bounced clear and spun off into the fog. The last he saw of his adversary was a white, steel wall disappearing into the shapeless void. He glimpsed a triangular transom and the jib of a stowed crane – then she was gone, to her accompaniment of threshing water and seething foam.

He yanked back on the starboard throttle and slammed both shafts into stop. The sudden calm was uncanny as she wallowed in the wash. His legs were trembling and he could not prevent the tremor in his voice.

'Sit still, Babs; and listen out while I inspect the damage. Yell for me, if you hear anything.'

He left her by the wheel, sobbing quietly to herself.

As he scrambled aft, a gull mewed, invisible, somewhere above him. To the northward, not far distant, a fog-horn sounded, booming through the fog.

CHAPTER 12

ss *Maori Frigo,* Container Ship

1510, Thursday, 3 June
Wind: Force 2, ENE
Visibility: 300 yards, decreasing to nil

Captain 'Thruster' Thirsk stood alone in his niche in the starboard wing of *Maori Frigo*, the ship's own wind ruffling his shock of red hair. He could pick out the after end of the fo'c'sle-head, but he was concentrating on listening for the nautophone of the West Hinder lightvessel. Because of the strong tides in the area, it was important to fix accurately at this point and he was keeping well south of the protective red, phosphorescent buoys. Then he heard it, a penetrating reed-like note, short-short-long.

'There she is,' he called to his navigator. 'West Hinder 1510. Note it in the log.'

He felt more at ease now; he liked a good departure from which to start and the next two hours were going to be busy. The ship had lost steam and the Chief had rung from the engine room to say that he needed twenty minutes to check the cause.

From the air-conditioned cell in the centre of the engine-room (for the benefit of the instruments, not for the comfort of the engine-room staff) the Chief and his team watched the control consol which monitored 690 different units of machinery. When one of these alarms sounded, the cause of the malfunction had to be rectified before the buzzer and the red light were eliminated. Working with super-heated steam from the two boilers which produced 32,000 SHP at 140 revolutions, the Chief and his staff had their hands full.

The breakdown had come at an embarrassing moment, when the ship was nosing past the Belgian fishing boats east of the West Hinder lightship. The incident had not been as dicey as when, in Wellington harbour, New Zealand, the ship had suddenly lost steam between two rapidly approaching ferries. He had shoved up a 'D' flag and used R/T on Channel 16. The ploy had worked a treat – both ferries had altered away at speed, like two naval destroyers.

The ship's fog-horn, automatically operated by the Seamac gear, reverberated from the fo'c'sle-head and the synchronized light flashed on the mast above the bridge – a sensible development which denoted the origin of the sound to other ships at night. He alerted the bow lookout, through the ship's communication system, to look out for the next buoy, the Fairy South, spherical, red and white.

He felt strung up this morning, tired after yesterday's passage in fog from Tilbury. He had had a plateful: unavoidably the inexperienced and uncertificated third mate would be the officer of the watch for the four-to-eight, when the ship passed through Piccadilly, the focal point off Sandettié where the shipping routes concentrated.

Thirsk could not insist that his only two experienced officers, the chief officer and the second mate, should be permanently on the bridge – they had their ship's duties to perform, particularly as the mate took over only yesterday at Tilbury. He was engrossed in trying to cope with the new crew and planning for the coming voyage to New Zealand . . . Thruster walked back into the wheelhouse, where the second mate was slapping a Decca fix on the chart.

Maori's wheelhouse was one of the best he had experienced – it was fully equipped with modern gear. If the radio officer had not mucked up the stand-by radar, Thruster would not have been so tense – the main set was okay, and God protect anyone who fiddled with the knobs again. Once he had lined up on a target, it was infuriating, time-wasting and dangerous when someone else tried to re-tune . . . brilliance, rain-clutter, anti-sea clutter, short and long pulse tuning, they all needed constant attention. Only experience could swiftly produce an efficient display just when it was needed – and today every possible aid was a bonus.

The pilot had been dropped at Akkaert and Thirsk was on his own. He liked it this way – no chance of a split command. The decisions were his alone. He had once had to share a hand-over with another master who was taking over the ship prior to Thruster going on leave – and that had been difficult, particularly as conditions had been very similar to today's. Each man had been sensitive of the other's feelings and decisions had been left to the other – fortunately the incoming master was a friend whom he respected, but when two men hated each other's guts, things could be positively dangerous. Thruster detested split commands.

No one, sometimes including the owners, could really appreciate the burden that a shipmaster carried these days. The split-second thinking required in these congested lanes, particularly with so many lunatics around, required acute judgement – and intelligent guesswork as to what the other chap was going to do. An error by any one master in a multi-ship confrontation could lead to disaster. Tiredness on the part of any one man; pressures from unscrupulous owners; minor health problems; or even perhaps temporary relaxation on the part of bored or stale officers – following the Saturday 'pub-lunch' routine, for example, when sometimes too much beer flowed. There were many reasons why, even in these congested waters, ships' officers of all nations were occasionally not as alert as they should be.

1531 – Fairy South buoy, three-quarters of a mile abeam to starboard . . . he poked his head into the radar: there were several echoes ahead . . . he would cross Piccadilly before it became even more congested.

'Steady on 271°, sir.'

The second mate was stirring himself today – normally, he lacked energy and was too often adrift with his chart corrections. Fixing the ship's position every ten minutes by Decca, checking the radar and keeping an eye on the new man on the wheel, used up every second – and now they were about to cross the lanes. Thruster preferred to cross as fast as was prudent, to cut down the risks – with *Maori*'s speed, no one could catch him, even if he had to turn her round and steer the same course as his adversary . . . At 1600 the bell rang, the watch changed, and the third mate took over on the bridge.

'Small echo passing slowly astern, sir – and a big chap coming up from the south-west in the deep draught route,' the new officer of the watch reported from the radar. 'There's a medium-sized echo on a steady bearing, two points on our port bow, sir.'

'She'll be coming up the north-east traffic lane to rejoin the deep-draughters at the north-east Sandettié buoy.' Thruster added, 'Keep an eye on her.'

He strode out to the wing again. He paused, watching the shadowy, arrow-like slivers from the bow-waves fanning outwards in their herring-bone pattern across the glassy surface. The phosphorescence glistening along the waterline was unusually pronounced this afternoon. This strange light behind the smothering fog-blanket was producing weird, sinister effects.

The visibility had lifted momentarily and less than half a mile on their port quarter the ghostly spectre of a white sail glided astern. He wished all sailing craft could act as sensibly – she must possess a good radar reflector. At least Rule 20 in the new 'Regulations for Preventing Collisions at Sea' went some way in helping the master of a big ship. A sailing boat could not now hamper a power-driven vessel navigating inside a restricted channel . . . that was one 'nonsense' the less.

'Stations' was sounding throughout the ship: the mate was an old hand and knew his stuff. The crew were scrambling into their life-jackets as they bustled to their boat stations. As Thruster watched them, a couple of starlings fluttered on to the deck abreast the funnel. They must be disorientated in this stuff; they would be surprised to find themselves in Liverpool . . . and then, away in the haze, he glimpsed the shadowy outlines of a small coaster and a monster Japanese container ship – both were well clear and steering for Hamburg, Bremen or the Scheldt.

'She's still on a steady bearing, sir.'

He returned swiftly to the wheelhouse and checked the screen: medium-sized ship, range 1200 yards and still closing on *Maori*'s port bow . . .

'There she is, sir.' The second mate had left his chart table and was peering through binoculars. A gas carrier, about 10,000 tons, steering straight towards – she had altered towards them even more, to speed up the rate of change of bearing.

'Stupid bastard. If she succeeds in hitting us, she'll go off with a bang . . .' Thruster muttered as he moved to the telegraph.

What was he to do? Hold on, as ordered by the regulations; chicken out and reduce speed; or alter course? Dare he leave the decision any longer, even if the man on the other bridge was one of those experienced cross-channel merchants who crossed regularly every other day? Admittedly, they enjoyed fine judgement, but they were presuming too much . . . he leaned across to yank the telegraph to 'stop', when the bearing began to shift across.

He watched her, a squat, ugly ship, pregnant with her spherical gas containers, as she swept across *Maori*'s bows – 600 yards at the most. In seconds, she had crossed and was displaying her triangular transom; in less than a minute she had disappeared in the mist that was clamping down again.

The background whine of the machines was the only sound on the silent bridge and then the hooter blared.

'Sandettié north abeam, sir.'

'Thanks . . . ninety-five revolutions.'

Things were moving too fast: that son-of-a-bitch was an example of the irresponsibility of ruthless operators. Piccadilly was too congested this morning – the plotting was becoming too fast for the bridge personnel. Sixteen knots was a better speed – more time to think, provided he crossed before the other shipping poured through this bloody awful spot. It was about time that the maritime nations organized themselves, as had the airline operators.

The wind across the bridge screen decreased and the bow-waves broadened. Visibility dropped to nil as *Maori* charged across to the separation zone.

A fog-horn, broader on *Maori*'s port beam sounded louder – she too was on a steady bearing, now that Thruster had slowed down. Would her nerve hold? If she held on, she would pass close ahead – but since *Maori* had reduced speed, what would she do?

'Starboard twenty.'

He was taking no chances. He felt better as soon as *Maori* began swinging – he would bring her round to a parallel course if necessary and wait for the large echo to pass ahead. *Maori* might have to stop, but at least he had taken bold action and had acted in time, so that she would not impede the deep-draught route.

There was the possibility of collision at this moment – the second in as many minutes. The approaching ship could not alter to starboard as the regulations required of her, because of the Sandettié bank – and she would take three miles to stop. If Thruster had held on as was his right, collision was certainly probable – yet *Maori* was obeying the traffic separation rules by crossing almost at right angles.

The ship's hooter blared above his head as he watched the helmsman ... 350° – North – 020° – 040° – 065° ... *Maori* was opening the distance.

'Stop the engine.'

If he did not slow down, he would be entering the north-east lane again ... the vibration eased and the deep boom of the big ship's fog-horn seemed much closer – it was impossible to judge the direction of the sound ... He dived into the radar and there she was, her bearing beginning to move ahead. She would pass at less than half a mile when she crossed *Maori*'s stern.

'Midships – port twenty. One-three-o revolutions ...' He would thrash across the separation zone as swiftly as he could.

'Sandettié north buoy, 170°, sir.'

'What's the time?' he asked from the depths of the radar visor.

'1645, sir.'

Captain Thirsk sighed with relief: *Maori* was almost into the south-west lane. A big ship was coming down from the north-east. From the relative plot, she should pass close ahead of him, when *Maori* turned south-west at about 1700. He would keep as close to the centre line as possible to give the approaching ship sea-room at the Falls.

At 1756 Thruster Thirsk identified the blur of the north Sandettié buoy which marked the eastern edge of the north-east deep-draught channel. The main north-east lane joined the heavy stuff here, at the northern tip of the Sandettié bank which divided the north-east traffic into two. He had maintained a speed of twenty-one knots to cross quickly, before anything else arrived from either direction. The advantage of crossing 'westerly' was that the heavy traffic coming up from the west had *Maori* on its starboard bow and so had to give way. This was all very fine, but a VLCC doing eighteen knots had little sea-room inside the bank.

He breathed again when he reached the north-west Sandettié: in a few minutes he would be across the separation zone and up to F2 buoy. The radar plot was not too unpleasant: several schuyts and coasters, outward from the German ports; a medium-sized echo crossing ahead; and a big chap on his starboard bow. The last was thundering down the south-west lane at speed, but she was still three miles distant. Apart from a few small blips, probably yachts in a cross-channel race, it was safe enough to turn into the lane in a couple of minutes.

He heard the clanging of the Sandettié landfall bell buoy, F2, but he never saw it. He swung *Maori* round at 1705 and settled her on 224°. The load on his mind lifted as he reduced to ninety-five revolutions. The fog here was as thick as ever, but *Maori* was with the traffic stream and the worst was over ... the ferries and the hovercraft in the Straits could look after themselves.

At 1707 the tell-tale identification of the Falls racon echo showed up on the screen; two minutes later he heard the two blasts from the lightship's diaphone grunting every minute. From the loudspeaker at the side of the wheelhouse, someone was chattering on Channel 16.

'D'you want the Dover Straits bulletin, sir?'

He was moving out through the starboard doorway for a breather, but his third mate was tactfully reminding him of the 1710 broadcast.

'They can be awfully depressing. Switch on, though – there might be something interesting.'

The Straits could be full of broken-down fishing boats, rogues would be scattered from here to Dungeness – in his opinion, it was all somewhat feeble until there were real sanctions internationally agreed – and then they would need fifty-knot battleships to catch some of these bastards ... he squinted into the bright glare from the haze ahead. Steaming westerly in the afternoon was a disadvantage because, if he sighted a ship to starboard, its wrong bow was lit up by the sunlight and invisible – it was easier when conditions were reversed.

was /

The sea was a steely grey where it merged along the invisible horizon into the yellow-tinged sky. The ship ahead of him, fine on his port bow, was leaving her slick in the oily calm; the sea shimmered along the pale path cast by the invisible sun. The bridge was silent save for the pounding of the engines and the roar from the air intakes – and every two minutes his fog-hooter blared its warning from the invisible fo'c'sle-head 600 feet ahead. His unseen neighbour, at seven cables on his starboard quarter, retorted with her low, booming fog-horn. She seemed to have reduced speed also, and was steering a parallel course.

'All ships in Dover Strait – this is Dover Strait Coastguard...' The officer of the watch had switched to Channel 10. Now to hear the worst ...

'Report number seventeen for 031710 GMT. General Information ...' Perhaps there might at least be something cheerful about the vis ...

'Extensive fog patches will be encountered throughout the Dover Strait. Visibility under two miles and this broadcast will be repeated at twenty-five minutes past the hour.

'One VSL at anchor in position two decimal five miles southeast of Beachy Head. A VLCC draught sixty-six feet is in position 355° Cap Gris Nez six miles course 050° speed ten knots. A wide berth has been requested.

'Seven canoes, accompanied by escort, crossing from Dungeness to Boulogne.' Thruster groaned. If they were stupid enough to attempt such foolhardy stuff, they would have to take care of themselves.

'Traffic Information,' the broadcast continued. 'In the southwest lane ship track letter Golf Delta is in position 330° Sandettié lightvessel –' Thruster pricked his ears, as he absorbed the positions – 'four decimal six miles, approximate course 080°, approximate speed twenty knots ...' The rogue was close ... 'This course does not comply with Traffic Regulations. Ship track letter Foxtrot Charlie' (one of the French rogues) 'is in position 245° Sandettié lightvessel five decimal two miles course 015° speed ten knots. This course does not comply with Traffic Regulations. This is Dover Strait Coastguard – out.'

Captain Thirsk put the telegraph to 'stand-by'. He crossed to the rear of the navigation island and peered at the chart ... the second rogue could cause trouble in ten minutes, but the first was a menace and too bloody close, if the coastguard was correct ... *Maori* was still too far to the eastward to have to worry about the Dover ferries whizzing across all day long, and they looked after themselves. He crossed over to the radar and thrust his head into the visor.

The picture etched itself into his mind: his large neighbour was still in station 700 yards on his starboard quarter, between the Falls and *Maori*. Fine on his port bow, were the two smaller echoes which he was overtaking, one 1200 yards ahead and further to port than the other, but close to the southern edge of the south-west lane.

He remembered glancing at his watch: twenty-six minutes past five. There was another blip, faint, a blur more than a definite paint on the PPI and disappearing inside the clutter. When he switched to close-range, the echo was fine on his starboard bow and closing fast ... three hundred yards at the most.

There was little he could do. He dared not alter to starboard with that big ship coming up his kilt on his starboard quarter ... he had two miles sea-room to port and he was still astern of the small stuff ahead – he would have to risk running into the north-east lane ...

'Hard a-port,' he rapped. 'Stop the engine.' He pushed past the third mate and shoved the telegraph to 'stop'.

Nothing of the echo now, not even a smudge.

He hurried to the starboard wing.

'Steady 180° . . .' There were only the wreck buoy and two

76

big echoes coming up from the south-west to worry about.

He felt the list as *Maori* began to swing. He peered into the swirling fog. *Nothing.* He ran to the starboard rail, leaned over the bow side-light – nothing but the roar of the wind and the seas smashing into her side as she swung. He thought he heard a cry down his starboard side, abaft the beam, but there was nothing visible in this stuff. He rushed back to the radar – still no echo . . .

'Ship's head?' he shouted. The helmsman should be on course by now.

'145°, sir.'

Thruster jerked his head from the visor. The helmsman, who had joined yesterday, was red in the face. He had lost his head as he tried to fathom the new bar-type steering arrangement.

'What the . . . ?' Captain Thirsk glanced at the compass repeater above the man's head. She was still turning to port but the swing was decreasing. The helmsman had followed the card round. In the emergency neither the third mate nor the master had noticed the man's error.

'Hard-a-starboard,' Thruster rapped. 'I have the ship.'

The card steadied, began to swing to starboard. He had her now; there was still way on her and she was coming back . . . She must be scraping the edge of the north-east lane; she was losing steerage way and the rate of swing was decreasing. He was shocked to see that seven minutes had elapsed since the emergency turn had begun.

'Slow ahead.'

The hooter was booming again and abeam he heard the reply of the big ship's fog-horn. She was passing swiftly up his starboard side, as *Maori* swung back to her original course.

'Note the time in the log . . .' Captain Thirsk said quietly: '1734.'

From somewhere ahead in the north-east lane, he heard an answering call from a big ship, low and resonant in the fog.

77

CHAPTER 13

ss *Niger Petrola,* VLCC

1727, Thursday, 3 June
Wind: Force 2, ENE
Visibility: 300 yards decreasing to nil

The master of *Niger Petrola*, Captain William Gratton, was disappointed he had been unable to sight the landfall buoy laid recently a couple of miles wsw of the Sandettié lightvessel. The phone call from his father had disrupted his concentration, but he would have been lucky to have spotted the buoy in this stuff.

After breaking away from *Bir-Hakeim* and weighing in that panic in Seine Bay, the pilot had contacted his station at Le Havre but they had heard no more of the unidentified trawler who had almost rammed them. The fog had cleared shortly afterwards, so he had cracked on up-channel at maximum speed. *Niger* had enjoyed a 1·2 knot tide under her, so she had made good seventeen, until he had been forced to reduce speed when visibility clamped down again off Le Colbart bank. He had nosed into the Dover Strait at ten knots, in spite of the faster speeds of others.

There was a lot of traffic in both lanes, according to the broadcasts from the Dover Strait Coastguard – and Bill Gratton was thankful to have the Le Havre pilot still with him. Trinity House would never have been able to fly off a helicopter in this fog – and a marine pilot via helicopter was an expensive luxury for the owners. He had never understood why they had built their de-luxe Pilot Station at Folkstone instead of at Boulogne; inward ships had to cross the lanes to ship their pilots.

In thick weather, Dover Coastguard broadcast at ten and forty minutes past the hour and the last broadcast had presented a dismal picture: the plot was littered with ships, but he had not sighted any canoeists. How could a foreign master without a pilot cope with this complexity? He needed a *Total Aid Chart* which would tell the navigator precisely what he was to do – instead of showering the bemused master with piles of bumph and inviting him to make his own choice.

Niger left the new buoy astern at 1727 and was coming up to the south-west Sandettié which was fine on her starboard bow. The coastguards had reported two rogues. The one which concerned him was already astern and crossing into the south-west lane. He had been watching her since 1630 when she had been abeam at three miles – she had passed under *Niger*'s stern by the MPC buoy at 1712.

Fourteen ships showed on his radar screen: two big echoes were following astern and *Bir-Hakeim* had been slowly overhauling since Seine Bay. She was now keeping station half a mile on *Niger*'s starboard quarter – Bill felt that her French master, Gael Le Bihan, deemed it discourteous to overtake in these congested waters and had adjusted his speed accordingly.

There was a small echo moving fast across the Channel, probably one of the hovercraft approaching across the Goodwins out of Ramsgate. He counted at least two possible Dover-Calais ferries crossing broadly across the lanes . . . and, to the northward, there were several small echoes – probably pleasure craft. A larger blip showed amongst them from the South Falls – perhaps one of the Boulogne-bound trawlers about which the pilot had moaned. Her bearing was moving slowly aft, but ahead, in the south-west lane, he had plotted at least five ships, belting on down, even in this visibility.

Fine on his port bow, and furthest away, was a small 'furry' echo merging with a large chap, due-east of the South Falls buoy. Between her and the separation line, with less than three cables between them, was another large echo moving at speed – probably one of the container ships from Rotterdam or Zeebrugge. She presented the most dangerous target – he would keep an eye on her. Ahead of her were two smaller echoes, small coasters probably, whose bearings were slipping safely down *Niger*'s port side.

The two big echoes were merging, the nearest at 5·8 miles – not far off at today's speeds. It had been demonstrated that under six miles it was impossible for two modern fast ships to avoid a collision, if the relative approach speed exceeded forty knots – a modern VLCC steamed at sixteen knots, had a turning circle of 1000 to 1500 yards and took six minutes to turn through 180°. A container ship could knock up twenty-eight knots; the relative approach speed could be over forty knots ... terrifying. These facts were a strong argument in support of father's hobby horse: his paper on a proposed *Marine Traffic Act for the Coast of Utopia* was already being happily adopted by some of the developing maritime nations of the Third World.

The Sandettié lightvessel was audible now – her siren moaned to the eastward, one long blast every half minute. If he had his way (and many of the younger masters thought as he did) he would install a gigantic control platform at either end of the Dover Strait, complete with pilot station, surveillance radars, directional M/F transmitters, marine police boats and helicopters, the lot. The international airports imposed their controls – why couldn't his own hidebound fraternity accept the discipline?

He could hear fog-horns all around him, large and small, distant and close. He had had enough of this congestion and would heed good old Regulation 16.

'Six-o revolutions,' he ordered. He turned to his navigator: 'Let me know when she's down to six knots.'

He strode across again to the radar as a fog-horn, nearer now, sounded again right ahead; the Sandettié sw starboard-hand buoy was coming up abeam. It would be passed at under half a mile, but he was loath to squeeze *Bir-Hakeim* who was still slowly overtaking now that *Niger* had reduced. He was worried by the situation developing so rapidly ahead ... What was that large echo, the probable container ship, up to? She had turned suddenly to port and must be well within the north-east lane. *There* – her hooter again – almost dead ahead. She was sounding off every minute, so must be in some sort of trouble.

'Sandettié south-west buoy abeam, sir. Our speed six knots.'

'Very good. Stop the engine.' He was forced to take avoiding action – the minutes had slipped by and the range had closed to two miles – her bearing was still steady and she was closing fast.

'I'll take her, Pilot. Starboard twenty. Steer 040°.'

He could feel the tension on his bridge. He could not help it if the pilot felt aggrieved – the final responsibility was with the master. If only he could use a sound signal to denote his turn to starboard.

'Call up *Bir-Hakeim* on Channel 16,' he snapped. *Niger* was squeezing the Frenchman on to the Sandettié south-west. 'Pass her my headings and speeds.'

He watched the compass card swinging, bloody slowly it seemed. Three minutes elapsed before she steadied on her new course. Gratton's head was buried in the radar, but he could hear from ahead the boom of the approaching fog-horn – the big echo was at 0·9 miles and the wreck buoy between them at only two and a half cables.

'Full astern.' He would take off *Niger*'s way . . . there was little else he could do.

The deck vibrated as her engine went astern. 'Two prolonged blasts,' he ordered, as soon as she had lost way. 'Note the time: 1739.' At least *Bir-Hakeim* would know that she, *Niger*, was stopped.

'Course, sir, 040°.' The Chinese helmsman seemed unconcerned.

'Can't raise *Bir-Hakeim*, sir. There's too much traffic on Channel 16.'

In the silence Bill Gratton slipped out to the side of his bridge. Two fog-horns were booming: one, mercifully, broader on his port bow – the other passing close up his port side. The sound reverberated in the dense fog and was very close.

CHAPTER 14

ss *Bir-Hakeim,*
Lightening Tanker

1728, Thursday, 3 June
Wind: Force 2, ENE
Visibility: 300 yards decreasing to nil

Captain Le Bihan had remained on the bridge since the fog had clamped down at 1430 off Cap d'Alprecht. He had lost three-quarters of an hour on *Niger Petrola* after they had broken away at 1000. The pilot, an old friend now living at Le Havre, had tried to discover on VHF whether there were any reports from a damaged trawler, but the Pilot Station had received no emergency call. Communications had been bad, because *Bir-Hakeim* was at extreme VHF limits with Le Havre; Le Bihan had remained in the area, until he was assured that no one needed assistance. *Niger Petrola* had gained six miles on him and *Bir-Hakeim* had not caught up until the fog worsened at 1430. He had gone to 'stand by' and reduced to twelve knots, until he had slowly made up on the Liberian.

Gael Le Bihan's stocky figure crouched in the port wings, as he tried to sight the new landfall buoy south of the Sandettié southwest. His eyes ached from staring into the shapeless horizon, but he had seen nothing visually. He would remain a good boy and observe the cautions on the chart; he would not overtake but would remain on *Niger*'s starboard quarter until they were north of the Falls. He would then pass ahead of her and get well up to the north-east, before crossing the south-west lane for the Outer Tongue and Longsand Head.

To make his berth at evening high water tomorrow, Friday, he would have to be under way from the Tongue deep-draught anchorage by 1600. To be certain of being included in the queue up-river, he was supposed to pass his Notice of Intended Movement twenty-four hours in advance. He had foolishly left his phone call until last thing and his radio officer had been unable to obtain an early link call. He had tried to get through on 16, but that frequency was as difficult. *Bir-Hakeim* was call number fourteen which meant at least another hour's wait. Everyone's arrangements had been thrown out of gear by the fog, so the radio telephone service was choked to capacity.

He hoped Universal's Marine Superintendent had been able to square the Harbour Master who was reputed to have a heart of stone . . . If the refineries had not been in desperate need of crude at the moment (a combination of Middle Eastern astuteness and a surprise demand by the summer holiday market caused by sterling's new-found strength) *Bir-Hakeim* would not have been allowed up tomorrow.

The Thames Navigation Service ran the Thames efficiently – it was the image of their dock labour that let the English down, rightly or wrongly. In comparison, Le Havre was an efficient port and jealous of its reputation.

The Thames Navigation Service needed accurate information to produce its planned passage diagram, so that it could successfully control the progress of deep-laden ships up-river. Le Bihan decided to try the link call again when North Foreland was less busy. Once he had cleared the bottleneck of the Sandettié, he could breathe again – the pilot, a competent man, could take *Bir-Hakeim* on up by himself. The man was an enthusiastic supporter of the Standard Operating Vocabulary which the English had produced – ships of all nations could now understand what was going on. The pilot was a helpful type; if pilots eventually became representatives of the port authorities, Le Bihan hoped they would all be as good as this one.

The captain strode back into the wheelhouse. Cap Gris Nez had just broadcast its CROSSMA information service in French and English on Channel 11. He would check the plot again, identify the rogue, then slip past *Niger* as soon as he could.

The Liberian was 0·8 miles ahead, her echo large and firm. The rogues were passing clear, ahead and astern, and they would not worry him; nor would the hoverferry cracking across from Ramsgate, but, *mon Dieu*, the screen was a mass of echoes – a nightmare to anyone unlucky enough to be in the Pas de Calais at this moment. Ferries were crossing at speed in both directions; rogues were ignoring the traffic routing regulations; a new buoy; and damned fool yachtsmen who had no business to be there in this stuff.

There was, in his view, an overwhelming case for obligatory traffic control here, controlled by the French and the English. Why could not leader-lines be used, as were laid on the seabed in the war? Then, ships fitted with galvanometers followed the cables wherever they led: in wartime through minefields; now, through the traffic lanes. Once you were on the circuit you remained on it, at a constant speed, until you were told to break off.

The airports did virtually the same thing; the congested air lanes had compelled air traffic control, and the operators had accepted the disciplines without question – they had no choice.

His head swam from the strain of staring at the PPI. He could count over seventeen ships in all; but his main two worries were the proximity of *Niger Petrola* who might squeeze him at the south-west Sandettié – and a fresh echo on his starboard bow, which had turned short of the Outer Ruytingen west buoy. By the speed of her relative movement and her course, she must be one of the Ostend or Dunkirk ferries. Wearily he marked her position and the time, 1728, in chinagraph pencil across the PPI. He straightened his back and moved out again to the port side of his bridge.

He was overdue for leave and in need of it. The demands made upon the masters of these large ships were becoming burdensome as the years flashed by and the congestion increased in the Straits. There was a chance that the nations might pull themselves together before too terrible a disaster befell, but he doubted it.

If the Pas de Calais was becoming a nightmare, what were the areas such as the North Sea and the Celtic Sea going to be like? It was bad enough already threading your way through the platform-studded areas – what would it be like in a few years time, if there was no obligatory routing and control?

Bir-Hakeim was slipping past the wreck four cables to the northward when the Sandettié lightship's siren wailed on his starboard hand. Fog-horns were blasting round the horizon, but Le Bihan was concentrating on his friend close on his port bow. At 1737, Captain Le Bihan first appreciated that *Niger Petrola* was reducing speed. At 1738, he registered that *Bir* was overtaking rapidly. Half a minute later he realized that *Niger* was altering to starboard. The clock showed 1738½.

'She's going to squeeze me,' he muttered. '*Merde* – what's she playing at?' There was little space between her and the Sandettié south-west: *Bir* was about to be nipped between the VLCC and the buoy. As he rang down to the engine room for 'stop', two prolonged blasts boomed through the fog: *Niger* had stopped and was making no way through the water. She was only four cables on his port bow and the bearing was unpleasantly steady . . . and *Bir-Hakeim* was still making eight knots.

'Starboard twenty,' Le Bihan snapped as he took over command from the pilot. 'Half astern. I'll shave the buoy close down my port side. I'd rather sink the buoy, pilot – *Niger*'s too big.' If he kept his nerve, there was just water enough between the buoy, the lightship and the tail of the Sandettié bank for *Bir* to slip through.

He moved to the helmsman's side and watched the compass. There was silence in the wheelhouse, nothing but the ticking of the gyro as the card began to swing.

'Steady on 068°,' he ordered. 'Tell me when the lightvessel is abeam.'

He would alter back to 041° and crack on speed as soon as he dared, to pass ahead of *Niger*.

'Range of *Niger*?'

'Four cables, captain.'

'Course, sir, 068°,' the officer of the watch reported.

Le Bihan moved swiftly to the port wing and peered over the side, watching the water while the ship lost way.

'Sound two prolonged blasts,' he shouted.

'Sandettié's abeam, captain,' the pilot called from the wheelhouse. 'There's an echo detaching itself from behind the light-vessel. Steady bearing and closing rapidly – could be that ferry we had on the plot a few minutes ago. *Niger* is passing clear down our port side.'

The chart table showed exactly 1740 as the two blasts of the hooter, punctured by an interminable second of time between them, shattered the fog swirling above the bridge.

'Ship has lost steerage way, sir,' the helmsman called.

He was clearing the VLCC though he was running out of water, and only bold action could avoid collision with the ship running in from starboard.

'*Emergency full ahead,*' he rapped. Once clear ahead of *Niger* he would alter back to port.

He strode back through the wheelhouse and out to the starboard wing. The siren of the lightship grunted and then another fog-horn blared. It sounded close and was broad on *Bir-Hakeim*'s starboard bow.

CHAPTER 15

MV *Castello de Sierra*, Coaster

1734, Thursday, 3 June
Wind: Force 2, ENE
Visibility: 100 yards

Since 1712, when he had altered course after almost running down a red can buoy marked 'MPC', Skipper Gonzales Zapiola had been slipping from his euphoric crest into a trough of despondency. The effects of his energetic forenoon and the alcoholic lunch with his woman had almost worn off; he was left with a foul temper and a mouth like a dirty doormat.

He had altered to 015° at the 'Milieu Pas de Calais' buoy, as soon as the sound of the fog-horns of the two big ships, bound up the north-east lane, had nosed ahead. They had been on his starboard bow ever since – impossible to judge the distance, but probably about three miles. He had been keeping his dead reckoning since the buoy and he judged he was now, at 1734, entering the south-west lane. He would remain at ten knots to cross as rapidly as possible. If it had not been for the crass incompetency of his drunken radio operator, he might have had something from the radar by now . . . He would have to continue using his ears – and in his rage he kicked the binnacle pedestal as he marched out again to the starboard wing.

He could not yet pick out the Sandettié lightship's siren – *Castello* was encircled by fog-horns: something large was approaching from the north-east and two more were sounding off to port and seemed to be opening their distances. He thought he heard a fainter fog-horn ahead, but at that moment the wheelhouse door slammed open. His radio man swayed in the doorway, filthy in his woollen jersey, the drunken fool.

'I've got the radar working, Skip. On long range only, but it's the best I can do.' That ingratiating smile of his was creasing his unshaven face.

' 'Bout bloody time.' Gonzales scowled at the unreliable man. He'd been slung out of his last ship and the agent had forced him on to Zapiola, to conform with the law. 'Can I depend on it?' He shoved his way past the blue-chinned Spaniard.

'The ship's heading is suspect, but the ranges and bearings should be okay. I told you before, you can't use short range.'

Zapiola's anger flared at the man's impertinence. He took a swipe at the grinning face, missed and lost the skin off his knuckles against the bulkhead. He swore and kicked the operator back through the doorway.

'There's a link call for us through North Foreland radio, Skip. They're calling us on the traffic list.' Smirking, the Spaniard disappeared back into his cubby.

Zapiola plunged his head into the visor of the radar as the helmsman yanked at the fog-horn lanyard. '*Christos*!' The screen was a mass of echoes . . . he tossed the stub of his cigar through the doorway and glared at the complex picture.

The shipping in the south-west lane into which he was now steaming resembled a trail of ants. He counted seven ships in each lane, two of them big, and coming down from the north-east. He must watch them. A faint small echo was crossing astern of the big ship; it bore a trail at its stern and was moving fast. It was on his port bow . . . he whistled as the strobe swept round again.

The two ships he had followed for so long were approaching the Sandettié lightvessel and there was a smaller echo to the east of them crossing to the westward. *Castello* was safe enough, though there was something coming down through the Falls – could be one of his Boulogne friends.

'Message for us from the agent, Skip.'

Gonzales raised his head from the radar screen. The radio operator was holding the message sheet for him to read, but the paper was shaking and difficult to read.

'What's it say? Read it to me, idiot.'

'*Castello* is to divert to London Docks and load to capacity with scrap. Then we are to proceed to Middlesborough as scheduled. Time of receipt 1738.'

Zapiola swore. He had never been up the Thames; the ship could not load much more before being down to her marks. Greedy lot of bastards. They had even complained when he had insisted upon a complete outfit of chart folios for the British Isles. He glanced again at the screen before moving out to the port side to listen to the fog-horns – he was feeling happier now that he was well into the lane and heading for South Falls buoy.

The fog was condensing on his eyebrows and moustache as he screwed up his eyes, trying to distinguish sea from horizon . . . all round him was this impenetrable dense blanket. He turned to listen to starboard: the low note of a siren moaned on his beam – he would stop the ship and catch it again at the next half minute, for that was the interval the manual gave for the lightvessel . . . He knocked the telegraph to stop.

He held his breath; the pounding of *Castello*'s diesels and the thud of a block swinging free on the fo'c'sle-head made things difficult – but then he heard the two fog-horns again, broad on his starboard bow, but fainter.

As he waited for the Sandettié's siren to wail again, he was surprised by a strange sound increasing from his port bow. He turned to listen . . . this was something he could not identify, a mounting crescendo, growing suddenly very loud. No ship made such a noise . . . No bow-wave, no thundering diesel – and then suddenly the air about him was vibrating.

'*Full ahead both engines!*' Zapiola yelled from the wings.

A cataract of sound overwhelmed him. From out of the sickly, yellow fog, a grey shadow loomed.

Adolfo, the helmsman, had not heard the order. His mouth hung open and he stood immobile clutching the spokes of the wheel.

'*Full ahead*, Adolfo!' the skipper screamed again in exasperation. '*Hard-a-starboard.*'

A wall of spurting spume, a grey curtain ten metres high leaped towards the helpless coaster. Zapiola heard a strange, high-pitched whine above the roaring cacophony, and then the spectre vanished, slipping swiftly across his starboard beam into the impenetrable fog.

Zapiola staggered back into the wheelhouse. He was trembling and his mobile, flabby face was ashen grey.

'Port twenty', he muttered. 'Bring her back to 015°, Adolfo. I'm getting outa here.'

CHAPTER 16

Hoverferry
Watson Watt

1734, Thursday, 3 June
Wind: Force 2, ENE
Visibility: 100 yards

The trip was proceeding nicely. Captain Jones, perched high in
his seat on the bridge of hoverferry *Watson Watt*, was feeling less
cantankerous as he steered his craft at fifty-two knots across the
south-west lane. So far, so good, in spite of the nil visibility.
Kemp was performing satisfactorily, though his obvious nervous-
ness was only to be expected.

'Resume course 131°, sir. We should pass well ahead of the two
south-west bound ships on our port bow. The north-east traffic is
well clear, sir.'

'Very good.'

Captain Aloysius Jones had steered for the hole between the two
big ships coming down the centre of the south-west lane. They
had remained invisible in this fog, and inaudible too, in spite of
their fog-hooters; the roar from engines and the pounding of the
hull drowned all external sounds.

The intercom between Kemp and himself was giving no trouble
today. He had crossed the Goodwins normally and had picked up
on the radar the other company's UK-bound hovercraft, passing
on opposite course clear to the southward. They were a good lot
and had been helpful, even though Hoverferries had been inter-
lopers and were now competitors. The tracks of the two companies
were routed well clear, because of Hoverferries' initiative in

building their hoverport to the eastward of Calais: by steering for the Dyck lightship, there was no collision hazard. The new land-fall buoy had been laid to help the hovercrafts and he particularly wanted to identify it. He had been baulked by the visibility for days, but today he meant to find it . . . Kemp should be picking it up at any minute.

'Where's the new buoy?'

Kemp's hesitance grated on Jones's nerves.

'Not a hundred per cent sure, sir. Could be very fine on our star-board bow. I thought there were two echoes, one closer than the other. Sandettié south-west well clear, 2·6 miles, 088°.'

'Which is the new buoy?' Jones tried to conceal the irritation. He must give Kemp a chance. Damn it, he, Jones, had made mistakes – but he had never covered them up; he would never have got away with it, with the masters he had served.

'There's little change of bearing from either, sir. One of them could be a yacht. They're close together.'

The roar of the craft and the bucketing increased suddenly as *Watson Watt* crossed somebody's wake. Jones gripped his control column.

'Distance between the echoes?'

'Less than a mile now, sir.'

'Take me close to the first.'

'Aye, aye, sir. Ten degrees to starboard. Steer 141°.'

Jones eased her round, watched the course settle on the Track Recorder.

'When should the buoy come up?' he rapped. He glanced at the clock above his head: 1739.

'Any mo . . .'

Captain Jones never heard his navigator's reply. A sudden quickening of his personal built-in warning system was alerting him to something he could not explain. He felt the kick in his stomach as, through his windscreen wipers, the fog seemed to thicken. An indistinct shape loomed through the glare . . .

'*Emergency turn to port*,' he rapped, nodding to the chief officer at his side.

He wrenched the craft round, sensed the chief officer knocking back the pitch. As the deceleration flung him forwards into his straps, a shadow swept close down his starboard bow. Then it careered off into the mist of his frothing spume. *Watson Watt* listed suddenly to starboard, burying her nose into the sea as she slammed to a stop.

The duty electrician was snatching the chance of replacing a lamp in the defective police light on the starboard side of *Watson Watt*'s car deck. This was an opportune moment in which to carry out his routines, because passengers were banned from the car deck during passage.

The police light was in an awkward spot, immediately above a cluster of motor cycles that had been lashed to the bulkhead. An old Dormobile, chocked high with camping gear, barely left space for him to squeeze through in order to reach the thumb screws.

He was threading his way past the nearside wing of the Dormobile when he was flung forwards and flattened against the handles of one of the bikes. He gasped as the sharp metal jabbed his stomach. He doubled up with pain, trying to regain his breath. What the hell was the Old Man playing at, throwing her about like this?

The cars were waltzing up and down on their springs as the hoverferry lunged to starboard, then slumped to a stop. The Dormobile broke free and crashed into the cars on its off-side. It slithered towards the bikes and he flung himself clear. He fell and his head banged against the deck.

As he rolled free, he glimpsed a flickering blue trail streaking from beneath the Dormobile. There was a flash, and then an orange ball of flame enveloped the vehicle as it burst into flames.

He yanked himself to his feet. He rushed to the fire alarm as the car deck exploded into a raging inferno.

CHAPTER 17

MV *Ypres,* Cross Channel Ferry

1735, Thursday, 3 June
Wind: Force 3, ENE
Visibility: Nil

His navigator, the second mate, had brought the 1720 French CROSSMA broadcast to him in his cabin, where he had been dozing in his chair. Captain Paul Vanderhaguen had carefully absorbed the contents of the Cap Gris Nez Information Service: a gaggle of big ships was entering the Straits and they would be in the northeast lane just as he wished to cross to Dover. If he altered short of the Outer Ruytingen west buoy, he could cut rapidly across the Straits and reach clear water in the south-west lane before the congestion piled up from the south-west.

At 1728, Captain Vanderhaguen returned to the bridge, checked the position of his ship, *Ypres,* then altered to the north-westward on a course of 310°. He increased speed to twenty knots, left the mate in charge of the watch and told the navigator to man the radar. At twenty-five minutes to six, he went out to the port wing for fresh air and to listen for fog-horns and the siren of the Sandettié lightvessel.

The broadcasts from Cap Gris Nez and Dover Coastguard were a boon to the ferry captains. He relied on them, although, as so many other masters, he had at first been sceptical. The two rogues which had been reported were well clear of him – it was criminal stupidity on the part of a shipmaster to ignore the separation regulations on a day such as this – incredible – but all part of today's trends, he supposed.

94

He enjoyed being out in the wings on his own. On the whole his officers were a good bunch: they worked hard, one-in-three watches, one week on duty, one week off. The crew were a stable, middle-aged lot; it was difficult today to persuade youngsters to go to sea. He had a crew of twelve, also working one-in-three, which gave him four men on deck. They worked four days on and four days off, a system which they preferred.

Paul Vanderhaguen had once spent a short weekend in Dover with his English friend, a Trinity House pilot. When returning to the Continent via a Sealink ferry, *Ypres* had passed on opposite course, under the command of the Company's spare-crew master. She had looked fine, the fresh white paint of her hull and her orange upperworks gleaming in the sunlight, a bone in her teeth where the bow-wave frothed at her fore-foot. He had always liked her clean lines and her squat blue funnel; he preferred her classical silhouette to all those modern, tub-like monstrosities that were being built nowadays.

He leaned over the screen and watched the hardiest of his passengers promenading around the sun deck. The ship was crammed to capacity which made up for the slack winter period. Without the summer tourist, the company could not survive.

From the radar plot, there was little to worry about until he reached the lightship. There were several echoes coming down from the north-east and something was steaming up from the south-west. *Ypres* would pass ahead before he reached the Sandettié. The computer had declared that all was well, so that was all right, wasn't it?

If he had his way, he would prefer to put money into MF direction finding beacons, rather than computers. MF D/F ought to come first, then the computers could latch on to them. Every ship over 1600 tons was already compelled to carry a MF D/F set, so why not site beacons at key points to define the edges of the approved routes? On the English side, beacons on the Falls and Varne lightvessels could point the way for the main south-bound route; beams from South Goodwin and from Dungeness could define the limits of the inshore route.

On the French side, it would be just as easy to stream the shipping up the northbound lanes. If beacons were sited at Cap Gris Nez, East Goodwin, Sandettié and West Hinder, the control could be as good as that at London or Amsterdam airports. The hydrographers had only to shade these beamed lanes in suitable colours on the charts and even a punch-drunk Greek could not lose himself.

Paul Vanderhaguen identified the Sandettié lightvessel's siren, then strolled back inside his wheelhouse to check the radar before taking *Ypres* across the deep-draught lane. He preferred to leave the lightship close to port, passing between her and the bank; *Ypres* was thus shielded from the heavy traffic coming up from the south-west by the lightship and the starboard-hand Sandettié south-west buoy. He would not, at his speed, hear any fog-horns in the south-west lane yet.

He spoke to the mate whose head was poked into the Trumaster computer plot.

'What's your crystal ball tell us to do, Chief Officer?'

The mate grunted as he stared at the anti-collision system.

'A situation is developing two miles south of the Falls light-vessel, sir. There's a fast ship amongst that lot, but we should be across by the time she reaches the Sandettié lightship. The large echo in the north-east deep-draught lane has cleared the Sandettié south-west and will pass ahead. No collision situation exists . . .'

'What's her range?' The master was crouching over his radar and cross-checking the mate's observations . . . the lightship was coming up abeam and would pass at four cables. Using the chinagraph pencil, he noted '1738' against the position, as the Sandettié's dismal siren sounded close to port.

'One decimal three miles . . . a big ship, sir. VLCC.' Then, for the first time, he heard her fog-horn.

The mate had got it right. Once this echo had moved across, Vanderhaguen would alter to port under her stern, as soon as the Sandettié south-west was abeam. He would take no chances and would let the big fellow know where he was.

'Sound the fog-signal every minute,' he ordered.

He reached the port wing again as *Ypres*'s hooter throbbed from the funnel. As he stuck his head over the screen, a deep, prolonged blast sounded from ahead; then, a second later from the same ship's siren, another. The hooter seemed fine on his port bow – could be dead ahead – about a mile he judged, though direction and range were notoriously deceptive in fog. He would take no chances: there was a stopped ship ahead.

'Come down to twelve knots,' he ordered through the wheelhouse door. 'Note the time. What's her range, navigator?'

'Zero decimal nine, sir. Time, 1739.'

Ypres's fog-horn blared again, blanketing the lightvessel's siren. The fog was swirling across *Ypres*'s fo'c'sle-head and the halyards were slatting against the mast from the signal deck above. Then, from fine on his port bow, another hooter boomed: one prolonged blast, from a different horn – loud and very close; then another, a second later: two prolonged blasts ... from *Another* ship – between *Ypres* and the VLCC? Stopped and making no way through the water, right ahead ... ?

The navigator was shouting from the wheelhouse.

'There's another echo, sir, separating from the VLCC ... range, sir ...' He hesitated, while he turned to short range ... 'Range, sir, three hundred metres.'

Vanderhaguen dashed to the bow thruster control.

'Stop both engines,' he roared from the wing. 'Sound the fog-hooter!'

As the fog-horn died above him, a big ship's hooter boomed from right ahead.

'Hard a-starboard ...'

He slammed the power to the port thruster.

'*Full astern starboard engine!*'

He heard the tinkle of the telegraphs, held his breath for the vibration as she went astern. She began to swing to starboard. He stared across his port bow as the deck began to tremble. Then, for a brief instant, he stood rooted to the deck in disbelief, shaking his head.

A grey shadow was collapsing upon *Ypres* from out of the yellow fog above him. The looming, shapeless spectre became the recognizable shape of a massive bridge structure. Above *Ypres*'s boat deck a monstrous transom towered, swinging rapidly towards her port midships section. The knife edge of a tanker's quarter bore down upon the ferry which was still making headway. With a scything sweep, the tanker's starboard quarter sliced through *Ypres*'s upperworks, carrying all before it, mincing boats, davits and rails into fragments.

Vanderhaguen stood mesmerized, watching the huge ship bite deeper into the ferry's side; the tanker's quarter wrenched at the rubbing strake, the plating buckled, then peeled back like a sardine tin.

He heard the screams beneath his feet; his brain registered the report of exploding air when the car deck flooded and the bulkhead collapsed . . .

Vanderhaguen heard the screeching of twisting steel, saw the sparks shooting where the metal ripped. The tanker's quarter had sliced open the length of *Ypres*'s port side, from amidships to aft, along the waterline.

As he reached the wheelhouse door, *Ypres* listed suddenly to port, catapulted to starboard, then slowly settled back to port, the exhausts of her engines coughing from the funnel as crimson sparks showered skywards. '*Abandon ship!*' he yelled from the doorway. '*Abandon ship!*'

At that instant the tanker's safety valves lifted momentarily. The roar of her escaping steam drowned all else, but he saw the white face, the look of stupified incredulity on the mate's face, as *Ypres* heeled savagely further to port. An articulated lorry was hanging over the port rail. The screams of passengers filtered from the decks below, above the high-pitched shriek of escaping air. As she settled, with her starboard engine still racing astern, the radio officer was pushing out his Mayday.

'The duty-free shop's open, Dad . . . it's half past five.'

Guy Hannen took his son's hand and allowed himself to be hauled from his comfortable reclining seat. Ella was smiling, from seven rows behind him. Together they had decided to attack the queues; she would spend their last few Belgian francs on some toilet water for Gran, while he joined the baccy and booze queue already trailing around the corner of the Purser's office. Lucy, her chin lipping the top of the counter, stayed with her mother while Mark came with him, to fidget impatiently by his side.

This greed for duty-free always secretly shocked him, as he began perusing the faces around him, some impatient, others bored, but all mentally tussling how much they could afford at the end of their holiday. The inborn urge to win a few bob from the Customs drove the average man to stock up with more than he could afford or needed. All manner of men were represented in this queue: fat men from the industrial north in their late thirties; peaky old men from Lancashire; self-indulgent young men from the stockbroker belt in their middle twenties; the hard drinkers and the friendly professionals, the lorry drivers ... and Guy Hannen. Where and how did he catalogue himself?

He had been standing in the queue for five mintues: 1736 by the ship's clock and still the queue had not budged; Ella had finished at the perfume shop and was searching for him.

'Come on, Mark. There're too many people. We'll come back later. What d'you want to do?'

'Let's go on deck again. I want to see the White Cliffs.'

'We may not see them – fog's thick.'

'C'mon, Dad . . .' Mark was hauling him up the central staircase to the deck above. Campers and student holiday-makers sprawled across the steps, snatching at sleep. He caught Ella's eye and they all four moved out through the doorway on to the port side of 'B' deck. He led them for'd to the screen at the foot of the bridge structure. He drew Ella to him and she pressed close as he put his arm about her. She shivered from the clamminess of the fog.

'What's that, Dad?'

A diaphone grunted on the port beam. Hannen timed the duration interval; thirty seconds later, then, further aft, the fog-warning repeated itself.

'That's a lightship. From the chart in the saloon, I think it's the Sandettié.'

'Will we see the cliffs?' Mark was insatiable.

'Not unless this fog clears,' Guy said.

Dead ahead a distant fog-horn was sounding two blasts.

'B'rr . . . it's cold, darling,' Ella said, snuggling into his shoulder.

Through the opened window of the enclosed bridge above him he heard the 'ting – ting' of an engine telegraph.

'D'you want to go in?'

Ypres's 'own wind' was decreasing and it seemed quieter, out here in their solitude beneath the bridge.

'She's slowing down, Mark.' Then another hooter blared, deep, loud and sounding very close. He heard the telegraphs again and seconds later, the deck was quivering beneath his feet. *Ypres*'s fog-horn blasted above them, shattering the peace they had found.

He felt a prick of fear. *Ypres* was manoeuvring in fog, was slowing down, close to something big.

'We'll go inside,' he said, picking up little Lucy, 'It'll be . . .'

He never finished his sentence. A shriek of rending steel sounded suddenly from aft; a shower of sparks spurted upwards; a shock shivered the length of the ship – and then they were sprawling across the deck as *Ypres* catapulted from one side to the other.

Ella was calling to him.

'Look – above us, Guy . . .'

He stared up into the mist. A monstrous shadow was engulfing them – and then he made out a white superstructure and two vast blue funnels vanishing into the yellow sky. That was the after end of a bridge and the whole edifice was swinging towards *Ypres* – bearing her under, ripping her open. As he grabbed Lucy and Mark, he heard above him the tremor of panic in the commands issuing from the bridge – then the alarm bells were pealing.

'Stick close, Ella.'

He lugged the two children through the port doorway. He had one objective only – to grab those life-jackets he had earmarked last night during his solitary tour.

The alarm had ceased, but the loudspeakers were crackling, first in hurried French, then in unintelligible English:

'*Abandon ship stations,*' an intrepid hostess was broadcasting shrilly into the mike behind the glass screen of her office. '*All passengers report to their muster stations on 'B' and 'C' decks. Tous les passagers . . .'*

But the loudspeakers were drowned by yells of panic; and of women screaming as they cried for their children. The heaving mass was irresistibly sucked to the central staircase, the only focal point the passengers recognized. The passages and the central corridors were blocked by this flood of struggling, frantic humanity.

Sleepy men and women, half-dressed, some in their nightclothes, were stumbling from the couchettes and the cabins. Three men were fighting savagely for life-jackets, while a dazed officer was shouting instructions from a board which was knocked from his hands. Guy stretched out his arms to reach behind the door of the luggage rack, where last night he had seen a pile of life-jackets. He grabbed four and tossed them over his head to Ella. 'Get the kids outside, Ella,' he rapped. 'Wait for me on deck.'

He was trapped then by a horde of screaming school children surging along the passageway towards the forward saloon. Squealing for their 'Mr Carter', whom they had last seen in the bar, they scrambled and fought amongst themselves until the gangway was jammed solid.

Guy Hannen could do nothing. The panic swept through the terrified mob as it fought to reach the upper decks. He slipped backwards through the doorway as the ship heeled suddenly to port.

'I thought you'd never come . . .' Ella was standing by the rail and clutching the children to her.

He grabbed Lucy in his arms and rushed aft, Ella slipping and scrambling after him. He cut across the after sun deck, leaning against the list which was growing steeper at every second. He fought his way past the engine intakes which were still sucking air into the dying engine room.

The pounding of the diesels, the whistle blasts from the officers trying to regain control: these were the incidents that registered in his mind. It was every man for himself now – he was going to get Ella and his children into the water if it killed him.

'*Life-jackets*,' he gasped. 'I'll fix the kids, Ella.'

The orange jacket swamped Lucy; he would take hers with him and use it when once they were in the water. He flung his own over his head, jammed the other over Mark, telling Ella to secure the tapes as men and women stumbled past him towards the boats. A sailor was banging frenziedly with a hammer at the slips on the gripes of the nearest lifeboat.

'*Attention!*'

The gripes jumped free. There was a rush for the lifeboat, but it refused to slide down its ways as *Ypres* listed more steeply to port. Whilst they yelled, pushed and kicked at the boat, he managed to haul Ella and the children to the rail.

'Hold on for your life, Ella.'

The deck was slipping away beneath his feet, as he scrambled along it on his knees, searching for the life-raft cylinders he had spotted last night. A middle-aged officer was bawling through a megaphone from the bridge. He was pointing to the boats, waving his arms as he tried to control the panic.

Guy Hannen was fighting for life. One thought obsessed him – to find those life-rafts . . . Cursing his stupidity, he saw a couple of plastic cylinders stowed beneath the third lifeboat. Ella, with the kids encircled between her arms, was hanging on to the rail right beside the davit. He wrenched at the toggles on the cylinder and the lashings dropped free. He shoved at the container, saw its lanyard jerk taut, heard the air squealing into the rubber raft. As the boat inflated grotesquely, he glanced over the side to where water was curling along the red of the ship's anti-fouling. He kicked at the raft and sent it spinning into the sea. Grabbing Lucy and Mark, he pinned them to him as he hauled Ella after him.

'Slide down the side,' he yelled into her ear. 'I'll be right behind you.' She was hesitating, so he pushed her brusquely and sent her slithering down the side which was rolling up to meet them.

The raft was bobbing in the swell, held by its lanyard. Tucking the two children under his armpits, he straddled the rail. He felt the burn as he hit the rubbing strake – and then he was toppling into the sea.

'*Guy . . .*'

She was calling close to him and was already clambering over the rounded side of the inflatable. He swallowed a lungful of water, then thrust Lucy towards Ella's outstretched arms. Mark was floundering beside him, but he calmed the boy, then yanked him over the gunwale. Gasping and exhausted, Hannen grabbed a line and hung on. He remembered seeing the bottom of the ship gleaming in the cauldron; recalled struggling for the knife he had always carried since his naval days . . . He sliced at the painter and shoved with his feet against the barnacled plates of the sinking ship.

He kicked off with his legs, thrashing in desperation. *Ypres* was rolling over to port and now lay on her side, her plating sprinkled with ant-like figures hurling themselves into the boiling sea. One boat had got away, but it was upended in the water, its after fall jammed. An officer was hacking at the wire falls with an axe, but his frenzy was futile.

'We'll wait here,' Guy called from the water. 'We'll load all we can.'

He saw the children imitating their mother, as she stopped her ears from the screams of the injured and the drowning. A head bobbed in the water and an arm waved in supplication less than twenty feet away. With his free hand, Guy began paddling the raft towards the swimmer. In the distance, a fog-horn boomed; seconds afterwards, he heard the doleful grunt of the Sandettié lightship.

CHAPTER 18

ss *Bir-Hakeim,*
Lightening Tanker

1741, Thursday, 3 June
Wind: Force 2, ENE
Visibility: Nil
HW Dover: 1757
LW Dover: 0051

1741, Thursday, 3 June was to be scarred into Captain Le Bihan's memory for the remainder of his life. Less than a minute earlier, he had rung down for full ahead on his engine: he was already clear ahead of the stopped *Niger Petrola*, but he needed to cross her bows to port, in order to regain sea room and depth of water.

Seconds after hearing again the fog-horn close on his starboard beam, he ordered full port rudder to avoid the invisible menace. He had left the navigator on the radar to call out bearings and distances, so that he, Le Bihan, could listen in the starboard wing. He was standing motionless, his head cocked and squinting into the fog forward of the beam. The navigator had called out, 'Nine knots, ship's head 049°,' when there was a shout from the bosun who was supervising the greasing of the lifeboats' falls.

Le Bihan swung round. A grey shadow drifted towards his quarter. As he watched, the spectre leaped out of the fog, a white hull, topped by orange upperworks and a blue funnel.

Bir-Hakeim's starboard quarter bit deep into the small ship's beam. He glimpsed the sparks, heard the screeching steel, saw the agonized face of her captain, a midget figure beneath, staring upwards from his bridge.

'Stop the engine,' Le Bihan cried. 'Wheel amidships.'

Leaning over the side, he watched the edge of his transom ripping open a cross-channel ferry, for that was what she must be. Her plating peeled back and, in that second, he glimpsed the lights of the ship's car deck. The ferry was being rolled over, when suddenly she righted. She flipped to starboard, rocked back to port again, then took on a steep list. She was still under way and was driving herself under . . .

'*Mon Dieu*,' Le Bihan whispered. '*C'est affreux . . .*'

As suddenly, she vanished, devoured by the fog. He turned away, sickened, as his engine room alarm pealed. He rushed into the wheelhouse and grabbed the phone to the engine room.

'Chief, here, Captain. We're holed along the waterline – a five metre gash. We're making water fast.'

'Will you have to abandon?'

'I'll have time to shut down the boilers . . . That you, Captain?' Le Bihan could barely hear the chief engineer above the noise of the deluge in the engine room.

'Yes, Chief.'

'The monitors are registering losses from six and seven main cargo tanks. We're losing crude fast.'

'How long can you give me steam?'

'Less than ten minutes. There's residual pressure.'

'Do your best . . .'

'Right, Captain . . . We'll . . .'

The phone died. Le Bihan wound on 110 revolutions.

'Starboard twenty,' he rapped at the helmsman. 'Steer 070°.'

He nodded to the officer of the watch. 'Muster all hands to stations.'

The chief officer had already arrived on the bridge. He was out of breath, standing in the doorway. '*Monsieur*,' Le Bihan ordered, 'stand by to anchor under-foot. I'll try to beach her. Keep all hands at stations and in life-jackets. If the Chief can give me steam, we might reach the Sandettié bank.'

He felt the tremor beneath his feet as *Bir-Hakeim* gathered way again – the log was already showing four knots. It seemed an eternity since the collision, but the clock showed only 1744.

'Navigator, fix the ship. Give me the exact course for the eight metre patch on Sandettié.'

'Course, sir 070°,' the helmsman reported.

Le Bihan went out again to the starboard wing. The wind soughed against his face. With horror he knew that men, women and children had been horribly mutilated, were dying and drowning in that stricken ship. No one could reach her. What he had always dreaded, had become reality.

'Course for the eight metre patch, sir, 076°.'

'Steer 076°. What's my speed?'

Sparks was standing by him, a message in his hand.

'A Mayday, sir, from a hoverferry. She's on fire and abandoning. She gives her position as three decimal one miles west-south-west of us.'

Le Bihan nodded. He had his own worries.

'Speed, sir, seven knots . . .' the navigator called above the chatter of the VHF. The captain turned to his radio officer.

'Anything from the ship we've just run down?'

'No, sir.'

'No Mayday?'

'Nothing, sir.'

'Push out a PAN-PAN, giving our position at 1741. Report that an unknown cross-channel ferry may be sinking in that position; tell 'em I'll be making an amplifying report as soon as I can.'

The young man was slipping through the door of the radio room when the soundings began to run back.

'Twenty-six metres, twenty-four . . . speed nine knots,' the navigator reported. He was a calm one.

Le Bihan glanced at the clock: 1746. A few minutes and she should touch. In the background, he could hear the radio officer intoning his PAN-PAN-PAN. The loudspeaker in the corner was busy on Channel 16, but Le Bihan had no time to listen.

'Shut all watertight doors,' he ordered over the inter phone. 'Stand-by collision stations and fire parties.' He repeated the order and returned to the wings, as the phone buzzed again.

'Chief Engineer, sir,' the officer of the watch called out. 'He's shut down the boilers and is abandoning the engine room.'

The Master nodded. This was it. *Bir-Hakeim* would either reach the bank or sink.

'Eighteen metres, sir.'

'Speed?'

'Seven, dropping to six, Captain.'

'Time?'

'1747 . . .'

Her way might carry her far enough and he still had a touch of tidal stream under her – so long as he did not miss the bank. He would remain on 070° until he was sure he was over the bank – then, if he had not already grounded he would turn further to starboard. The bottom was sand; if he could judge it right, he would not hole her further.

'Four knots . . . Time is 1748, sir.'

He braced himself against the bridge screen.

'Fifteen metres . . .'

She would touch at any moment now – she would be drawing more aft, if the engine room was as bad as that.

Then, almost imperceptibly, he felt the way gently coming off her.

'*Let go starboard anchor . . .*'

He put down the mike and heard the rattle of the chain. The clanking ceased rapidly. The ship had stopped. He stepped to the wing and leaned over the side. The water was swirling along the water-line. Below him, and slightly forward, a spiral of black crude oil was welling to the surface of the sea. A few miles to the south-west a hoverferry was ablaze. The sea could be on fire.

CHAPTER 19

Dover Straits Coastguard

1743, Thursday, 3 June
Wind: Force 2, ENE
Visibility: 10 miles to northward; 100 yards on clifftop

The receiver in Captain Tuson's pocket began bleeping at 1729.

'Sorry, but I've got to leave you. There's an emergency developing.' He shook hands with the senior official from the Department of Trade, and scrambling over the debris outside the old gun emplacement at Fort Langdon, he jumped into the old 'banger' which was provided for his local running-about. He called through the window as he rattled up the road:

'This shows how much we need the new Operations Centre here. Hope you can find your way back ...'

Money, the eternal problem ... politicians could not see beyond the end of their noses. Did they have to wait for another disaster before money was voted for a fully equipped Centre able to serve shipping traffic in the Straits?

Dermott Tuson ground his foot on to the accelerator and forced the Volkswagen up the hill. He glanced in the rear-mirror: nothing following, but the face peering back at him was showing signs of strain.

These past months had been hard and his face was reflecting the long hours. The blue eyes were still steady, but the grooves between them bit more deeply into his forehead; and the lines at the corners of his mouth had lost their kindly humour. The conflict and the frustration with bureaucracy had left its mark.

His black, well-groomed hair was greying at the edges, but, at fifty-four, he still retained the crisp air of authority which his time in destroyers had given him. He was a neat, compact man of medium height. He was fit, and when he was in a hurry he moved fast.

His job as Inspector of the Coastguard at St Margaret's Bay had totally absorbed him. He had been selected for the job, he now realized, because he could get on with people. This quality (plus the fact that he had spent his childhood in the area) had stood him in good stead when dealing with local opinion – with his love of this part of the world, he could understand the fierce opposition to any despoilation of these incomparable cliffs.

Things had changed so rapidly: it had been impossible to arrive at the right conclusions without proper analysis – and this was where the National Physical Laboratory had been so invaluable. Without the NPL's systematic research, the Marine Traffic Systems Steering Group would never have been able to progress. Previously, the press had produced exaggerated figures of the traffic in the Straits but the NPL had now established proper statistics: nature of the traffic, composition, future trends of traffic flow, causes of marine casualties and the annual rate of collisions.

The aim of his Operations Centre was concise: to contribute to the safe and timely passage of ships through the Dover Straits and its approaches. To achieve this, his job was to provide an up-to-the-minute Information and Surveillance service. He had no powers to enforce traffic control and that was where his opinion differed from that of others.

His duty was to monitor, survey and inform shipping in the Straits. To achieve this he had to run a continuous plot of the ships' tracks and positions. He had set up a permanent record by instituting a twenty-four hour photographing of the PPIS. This evidence was vital when reporting rogues to their governments.

To collate his information broadcasts, he needed the help of the users of the Straits. His service could be no better than the information he received from the ships themselves, but he was tolerably satisfied with the way things were going. Ships passing through the Straits were now volunteering information on the weather, buoys off-station, mines and visibility.

His French friends in CROSSMA across the Channel at Cap Gris Nez were perhaps more logical . . . it would soon be compulsory for French ships to guard Channel 11, their broadcast frequency, when, at twenty and fifty minutes past each hour, they broadcast their CROSSMA service with an English translation. No French shipmaster could offer the excuse that he had never known of the danger.

Tuson did not like compulsion. Naturally, he did not report ships who could not conform safely with the traffic regulations which IMCO (the Inter-Governmental Maritime Consultative Organization) had instituted for the Straits. IMCO had adopted these traffic separation schemes owing very largely to the initiative of the Institute of Navigation through its director who had begun thinking fifteen years ago of means of alleviating collision risks in the traffic concentrations forecast – unhappily, the *Torrey Canyon*, *Pacific Glory* and *Achilles* collisions had proved him to be only too prophetic. Ships were beginning to accept the need for discipline; many of their masters were now reporting when they were unable to conform. Their thoughtfulness helped the coastguard and avoided unnecessary unpleasantness.

The ancient Volkswagen was labouring up the stony track . . . he wished it would get a move on, for the fog was bad here and they were needing him at the Centre. This could be the beginning of one of those days about which he suffered nightmares; disaster could strike at any time. Fog was the worst of the hazards, for those brought up with radar had forgotten the imperative need to reduce speed in these conditions. Fog was no new condition; he was not surprised when statistics confirmed that over eighty per cent of collisions took place when visibility was down to less than one mile.

The modern captain had such suffocating pressures thrust on him. His ship could take as much as three miles to stop. His route was plagued by irresponsible yachts; by fishing boats who were concerned more with what went on below the water than what was above it; and during the holiday season, either a hovercraft or a cross-channel ferry was crossing the lanes every two minutes – or 150 crossings a day.

He supposed that compulsion had to come. How could the maritime profession excuse itself from the incredible disaster a few years ago, when one ship, then a second, and finally a third (after steaming through sixteen buoys to do so) finally succeeded in colliding off the Varne?

The press had given a figure of 7617 rogues for 1975. His radar had tracked an average of twenty-five rogues per twenty-four hour day – 8126 a year during 1975. This astounding figure included the sixty per cent French trawler contribution which was now reducing rapidly. Excluding them, the figure still showed an annual contravention of an average of ten ships daily, or 3650 annually – and this was a twenty-seven per cent improvement on 1974.

Curiously the West Germans were the worst culprits, followed closely by the Dutch and the British. Nine British masters had pleaded guilty during 1975 and were fined. The batting order continued with Cyprus, then Norway, Liberia, Russia, Denmark, Greece, France. Sweden was the good boy.

He did not hold the view that shipping could be controlled as were aircraft. There were too many technical difficulties; the air world was three-dimensional, wherein radar could operate without hindrance. Aerial radar was not bothered by wave clutter and other unavoidable difficulties.

If things went on as they were, the conservationist lobby had a strong case to exclude VLCCs and toxic cargo carriers from navigation of the Straits. The NPL studies of the deep-draught route for ships drawing more than fifty-six feet showed that the regulations were being largely ignored by all ships, other than those for whom the route was devised. The problem of this route and of the notorious Sandettié-Fairy Bank area, had recently been discussed at a Hague meeting between Britain, France, Belgium, Holland and West Germany; recommendations had been submitted to IMCO and one day might become law.

Hopefully, things might move more quickly; the recent adoption of the new collision regulations (1972) had taken years, but at least Rule 10(d) demanded that ships hitherto passing through the inshore zones should normally use the adjacent main lane. This should have the effect of turning the English inshore zone into a lane for only north-east bound ships – but it was too early yet to tell.

Tuson's job was also surveillance – but there *were* moments when he would like to know what ships would be coming through. The ports and shipping authorities would benefit from an obligatory control based on the TRs which ships were already obliged to make to the various radio stations. If these TRs could be collated at some central station, everyone would know where he stood.

Perhaps the whole future lay in tying ships to a track and providing them with information – but all depended upon communications. Pre-war, the Atlantic passenger ships, particularly when in fog, broadcast their positions, course and speed to all adjacent shipping. The White Star mail-ship, bound west in dense fog on the Newfoundland Banks, doubled up her lookouts and knocked down three knots. She had to be off the buoy at eight o'clock on the Monday morning, or else . . . So she broadcast her intentions.

A modern ship, claiming to be a hampered vessel and needing total constriction, should do the same when she began to insert herself into the system. She *ought* to signal: 'Here I am. I am proceeding along route A and my speed of advance will be . . . I'll report if I'm not on track.' Your cross-channel ferry could not then claim ignorance.

The Volkswagen juddered to a stop on the cliff above St Margaret's Bay. The fog was thick, swirling in yellow gobs across the gorse-fringed edge poised above the invisible sea. Tuson slammed the door behind him and ran up the outside ladder leading to the ops room. He shoved open the door, as Pamela Hurst, the auxilliary coastguard, was ripping the Mayday from her typewriter.

'MAYDAY, MAYDAY, MAYDAY,' he read, '*This is Hoverferry* Watson Watt *in position* 270 *Sandettié lightvessel* 4·5 *miles. On fire and abandoning ship. Request assistance.* TOO 031742.'

In the background Dermott Tuson could hear the whine of the

machines, and, through one of the loudspeakers, the clipped voice of the North Foreland Operator trying to impose radio discipline. His calm authoritative voice was dealing with some foreigner who was continually breaking in on 2182.

He turned to his Duty Station officer.

'Institute Full Rescue Procedure.'

'Aye, aye, sir.'

The bearded officer nodded towards his team, a Grade I coastguard officer and two coastguard officers, when the radio cut in again on 2182.

'PAN, PAN, PAN,' (the accent was French and the operator was in a hurry) '*This is Lightening Tanker* Bir-Hakeim, *in position* 327 *Sandettié lightvessel, zero decimal nine miles. In collision with unidentified vessel, probable ferry, which may be sinking. I have been holed below waterline and will make amplifying report shortly.* TOO 031746.'

Tuson stood in the middle of his operations room, hands behind his back, listening to the drill which he had made his team exercise so often. Sadly, the last occasion for real had been the *Achilles* affair, when the frigate had rammed a tanker amidships – again, in fog. The coastguard was responsible for alerting the rescue services and already the alarm was being pushed out over the landlines: the lifeboats; the RAF, Manston, for their helicopters; the Dover police; the Ministry of Defence. Troubles certainly never came singly. In this visibility the RAF could be grounded; little search work by ships of any size could safely be carried out.

The lifeboat's maroons boomed below the cliff from Dover: those unselfish men would be rushing down to their boat, scrambling into their oilskins and donning their life-jackets. But in this stuff what could they do? It was all too reminiscent of a terrible night in 1941 between Dungeness and Folkstone, when a convoy had been caught in a minefield which had been laid in fog ahead of it by German destroyers.

Today, women and children were drowning in these wicked tideways ... he felt sickened by the criminal stupidity of the rogues who were the source of these needless calamities – and by the inadequacy of the traffic control. The clock showed 1753 and the R/T was crackling again.

'PAN, PAN, PAN . . . *This is* Bir-Hakeim, Bir-Hakeim, Bir-Hakeim, *in position south-west tail of Sandettié Bank, approximate position* 043 *Sandettié lightvessel one decimal five miles.*' The operator was trying to conceal the panic, endeavouring calmly to pronounce an unhurried English:

'*Have grounded forward in fifteen metres of water. Engine room is flooded and ship is holed across bulkhead between six and seven cargo tanks, starboard side. Serious crude oil leakage. Further report will follow after survey of damage. Ship in no danger yet of sinking or breaking up provided weather does not deteriorate. Request anti-pollution measures and all ships to keep clear. No trace of unidentified collision ship.* 031753.'

Tuson turned to the station officer.

'Alert the Harbour Authorities and tell 'em we need the sprayers.'

At 1755 Manston reported that the helicopters would remain grounded until further orders. At one minute past six, *Watson Watt* broadcast a second Mayday: her fuel tanks had exploded and the sea was on fire.

The Inspector glanced at the tide board: high water was at 1757. Mercifully, the south-westerly ebb would not begin to run off Sandettié before eleven tonight: with luck, *Watson Watt*'s fire might have burnt out (strange that her kerosene had ignited) – or there could be fearful consequences if *Bir-Hakeim*'s oil floated down on the ebb into *Watson Watt*'s inferno.

He would himself inform Stuart Gratton, whose task as the East Thames Harbour Master was tough enough already. The earlier he could be aware of developments in the Straits, the better for his traffic movements. *Bir-Hakeim* may well have been inward-bound for Universal's terminal and her stranding would inevitably disorganize Stuart's programme for tomorrow.

It was now 1805. The ops room had alerted all the local authorities and now he would get through to London. The Minister for Trade might wish to take part in decision-making himself, because events had the potential of developing into a national disaster if the weather deteriorated after the fog. The barograph was beginning to slide after its long 'high'.

Tuson would talk first to his opposite number at Cap Gris Nez –

their efforts must be co-ordinated, or there would be an even worse shambles.

The Dover phone was shrilling.

'All the fishing craft equipped with radar are being alerted, sir.'

Tuson nodded. It was bloody thick out there. He hoped to God there would be no more accidents – the foul up was terrible enough already.

CHAPTER 20

The Minister

2340, Thursday, 3 June

Nigel Hurst knew when to remain silent. He had been the Minister of Trade's personal assistant long enough to know when to be wary of the Member for East Weald's idiosyncrasies. Weary from the panic of the last few hours, he settled himself down in the corner of the official limousine which was heading the convoy of ministerial cars speeding down to Dover on the A2.

The man in the opposite corner had fought his way through the political jungle and, at forty-seven, Raymond Grubb had achieved one of his main ambitions. He had trampled up the career ladder, leaving the rungs strewn with half-used 'friends'. He had been Minister for fourteen months, having negotiated the crises and added to his stature. Few men understood Grubb's mercurial temperament, but Hurst had been the indispensable tool whereby Grubb had managed to weld his department into one of the most efficient ministeries.

The Minister for the Department of Trade had been guest of honour at the Scriveners' dinner, and it had been Hurst's unpleasant duty to summon his master for the present emergency in the Channel. The secretary had sounded perturbed on the phone, but when Hurst told him that the Minister was excusing himself from the dinner and had called a meeting in Whitehall for ten o'clock, the official had rung off, a happier man.

When the Hon Member for East Weald arrived in the ministerial office at four minutes past nine, Hurst had already summoned the heads of Departments. Grubb was put through to the Inspector of the Dover Straits Coastguard, a Captain Tuson, who had provided an up-to-the-minute situation report. The incident looked, as Grubb often intoned in the House, 'grave'. The Minister's future could well be decided by the decisions he was now being forced to take. The Inspector's call and the emergency Whitehall meeting swallowed over an hour and it was dark before the final decisions were taken.

The meeting had agreed unanimously that this affair was developing into a major emergency: 'incident' headquarters were to be set up immediately at the Dover Straits Operations Centre, St Margaret's Bay; a frigate, HMS *Cumbria*, was already steaming at utmost dispatch from Portsmouth; the RAF was standing-by with search aircraft and their helicopters from Manston; the Dover Harbour Board was co-operating fully; the Anti-Pollution Division was alerted; Trinity House was standing-by at immediate notice to lay wreck and warning buoys; but, like others, they could do little until visibility improved. The tugs were on their way down from the Thames.

The minister was slumped silently in his corner. Hurst closed his eyes as the cars were by-passing the Medway towns. He was unlikely to snatch much sleep tonight.

Captain Tuson had presented him, Raymond Grubb, with a clear picture of events in the Straits – it was agreeable to be addressed as 'sir' by a Captain of the Royal Navy. Most sailors voted Conservative, so it was all the more pleasant to talk to a man who could show respect to the opposing camp . . . Yes, the Minister admitted to himself, he, Raymond Grubb, MP, had handled things tactfully and firmly at the meeting. He always recognized that the professionals, and particularly the brotherhood of the sea, held politicians suspect – and at one moment, just over an hour ago, he had felt that he himself was in the witness box. His Marine Division had hammered out how best to cope with the danger, firstly, to life; and secondly, to the coastline if the tanker was stranded or broke her back.

He must get *Bir-Hakeim* off the Sandettié as rapidly as possible.

Though the tides were falling off, his advisers had told him there was little chance of her being neaped, unless she settled too deeply. Two years ago he had never heard of these terms, but he had done his best to learn the jargon and to understand the working of his Marine Division.

The only real opposition which his civil servants had encountered had come from that forthright fellow from Gravesend – the Harbour Master, East Thames, he called himself. Grubb's men wanted every available tug, every suitable craft which could deal with the situation, to steam at full speed for the collision area. The Dutch 'ocean-goers' were already on their way from Amsterdam, but our boys wanted to be there first. The PLA had been in a difficult position, but had supported Gravesend who had vehemently demanded to retain a few powerful tugs for tomorrow's movements – but, for God's sake, could not those stubborn master mariners recognize priorities? In the winding-up, Grubb had been evasive, saying that he would make a final decision in the morning, when the situation should have clarified.

He had sensed the resentment – perhaps because the fraternity had met so much opposition when they set up their Traffic Control of which they were so proud – and Grubb had reacted by showing that he, too, could be decisive. He had ordered an immediate anti-pollution alert; he had left them in no doubt that he meant to have as many tugs in the area as rapidly as possible, but he had also insinuated that, naturally, he would not denude the Port of London.

Grubb had definite views about oil. He was more interested in the riches beneath the sea, than the oil carried by tankers above it. It was the territorial limits protecting our oil fields which concerned him. He could not agree that France and Britain should assert their right to control the Dover Strait and so be able to ban the big crude carriers from using this seaway. The ultimate disaster could never happen with the modern electronics which ships now carried – at least, so he had thought until tonight.

He yawned as the car swung round Canterbury. The motorway was deserted now and Nigel Hurst was asleep. For one of those rare moments, Grubb had the chance to think in peace.

The International Conventions of the Law of the Sea had tried to find workable solutions to the problem of territorial limits but had failed. Britain and France were already in dispute over the boundary between Britanny and Cornwall, in the area through which one of the world's densest traffic streams passed. If production platforms were to be built there, a workable separation scheme must be agreed – and rapidly imposed.

There was an average of forty-five collisions annually between ships of over 1000 tons. In the southern North Sea and the Dover Strait, the average was twenty-three collisions between ships of all types and tonnages, during the first half of the year when visibility was at its worst . . . During the latter half, the figure fell to fourteen. It was heartening to be told that the collision figures had decreased wherever IMCO had instituted its separation schemes.

Politics, politics – any progress revolved around international cooperation, in the same way as London River found order only through its Statutory Act and Powers of Direction. For once, he agreed with the visionaries: organization and planning must be agreed before the advent of the hardware. Technical improvements developed every day, and if we waited for the perfect computer and the ideal radar, no scheme would ever start. Raymond Grubb, MP, would support those who meant to get a move on, in spite of the opposition.

He had admired that forthright fellow, Gratton, who, at a vital conference, had put the matter so succinctly when he had addressed the traditionalist opposition. He could see him now, leaning across the table and facing some members of Trinity House and of the General Council of British Shipping.

'We understand your conservatism, gentlemen,' he had said in that unassailable and friendly manner of his, 'we realize that we are knocking at very ancient customs. We don't want to control the ship *or* the masters. We say: "*Somebody* must control the *overall* situation." ' The meeting had been memorable.

That was why he, Grubb, had made his presence felt at tonight's meeting: he was determined to show the country that there was no shilly-shallying in his Ministry. He had inferred his resolution to the Press, but the PM had not been so impressed when Grubb had telephoned. 'Better wait 'till the morning before you make your dispositions, Raymond,' was all the help he received from the Great Man.

He glanced at the clock glowing on the chauffeur's dashboard: 2340. The headlights were blurring as the car neared the coast. In ten minutes they should be reaching Dover and the Hon. Member for East Weald hoped that the driver would know his way in the fog up to the cliff – Grubb had visited the Centre only once, when he had inaugurated its opening. Hurst was stirring in the corner; he was breathing through his mouth and the resultant gurgling was irritating.

Raymond Grubb had always been a PR man. Early in his career, he had learned the truth that communication between people was the basic requirement if any enterprise was to succeed. He had not realized that in the transport world also, communications were the heart of the matter – Captain Gratton had demonstrated this truth down at Gravesend, but he was a professional communicator. He had delivered a homily to a seafaring gathering and Grubb had never forgotten it.

The seaman, Gratton had suggested, could no longer give second place to technology; the naval architect was indispensable in the building of his modern ship; the navigator had to accept the aids of modern navigation wizardry; the electronic engineer, with his micro-arts, supplied the computery; and lastly, but most lamentably under-exploited, came the vast field of telecommunications. There were 212 million telephones used in the world for people to talk to each other. Rapid transport demanded instant communications – yet seafarers were still teetering on the edge of this fast-developing marvel . . . but it was the economist who held the key.

Scheduled and planned movement was vital to the shipping industry: a ship was built by her owners solely to earn money. If she failed in this function, she was sold, laid-up or scrapped. Regrettably, it was nonsense for the views of seafarers to bear more weight than that of the economists. These were the hard facts in this brutal world. If Grubb had his way, he would put economics and communications first and second – both would ensure worldwide, standardized Area Procedures. The container revolution had swept through the world, standardizing road, rail and sea transport – why could not Area Procedures and communications follow that example? How slowly was the planet groping towards order and efficiency? It was through trade and transport that the world stood a chance of survival.

His thoughts were dragged back to reality by the sodium lighting which illuminated the dual-carriageway winding down into Dover. Then the car was climbing out again, eastwards towards St Margaret's Bay.

'Wake up, Nigel. We're here.'

As he swung himself wearily from the car, he glimpsed the outline of an obelisk against the sheen of the moon behind the fog. It was thick, this stuff, cold and clammy. He hurried past a row of police and army communications' trucks and clambered up the steps of the Operations Centre. Captain Tuson, in shirt-sleeves, greeted him at the doorway.

Grubb was impressed by the quiet efficiency with which the coastguard had taken charge. The R/T was crackling with orders, and acknowledgements were being systematically passed.

'The lifeboat has just landed the first casualties, sir,' Tuson said. 'Six badly injured passengers and seven women and children were found in one lifeboat.'

'What ship?'

'*Ypres*, sir. Belgian car ferry. Sunk off the Sandettié.'

'Certain?'

The Inspector nodded. 'An offshore fishing boat has landed a couple of corpses. Covered in oil and badly burned.'

'The hoverferry?'

'Difficult to say. One of their reserve craft is standing by, waiting for the fog to lift. She daren't approach too close for fear of running down survivors beneath her skirt.'

'Has *Cumbria* arrived?'

'Yes, sir, but she has the same problem. She's "on-scene commander". We're worried about further collision.'

Grubb felt his inadequacy amongst these calm professionals. They knew, and only they, what it was like out there, groping blindly in the fog, listening to the pathetic cries from the water.

'What about the tanker . . . *Bir-Hakeim*?'

'She's being helpful, giving regular reports. She's hard on the Sandettié bank. Oil is pouring from her and the tidal stream is running south-west now, towards *Watson Watt*. Worrying, sir.'

'Explain, Inspector, please.'

Tuson looked at the end of his tether, but courteously he continued:

'If it remains calm, the fog is likely to persist; the spillages will move up and down on the tides which will give us a chance to mop some of it up. If the wind gets up, depending on its direction, the oil may be blown on to our coast – or across to France; and the tanker might break up. You can't win.'

A coastguard was broadcasting over the R/T, warning shipping to keep clear.

'It's history repeating itself,' Tuson said. He was shaking his head as he turned towards the radar screen. 'Look at that, sir. The area is stiff with rogues ignoring all our warnings.' His finger traced the courses of five small echoes thrusting through the danger area. 'What can we do?' Tuson asked. 'It's the *Achilles* and *Texaco Caribbean* episodes all rolled into one.'

Another collision was inevitable, but the coastguard could only warn and watch.

'What's the weather doing?' the Minister asked.

'Barometer's beginning to fall, sir. North Foreland forecasts rising wind tomorrow afternoon.'

'Where from?'

'North-east, sir . . . Force seven later.'

Grubb stood motionless, aware of the possible consequences, terrible if the gale developed.

'I've ordered all available tugs and craft to the scene, Inspector. We've got to get that tanker off.'

He moved outside, suddenly very tired . . . Wisps of fog were drifting across the moon, a delicate tracery and very beautiful, if the night had not been so loaded with menace.

CHAPTER 21

Alouette, Trawler

0233, Friday, 4 June
Wind: Force 3, NE
Visibility: 110 yards

This hour was always the worst for Skipper Jean-Pierre Le Villain, of the Boulogne side-trawler, *Alouette*. Between two and three in the morning was agonizing, for he always had to combat the onset of sleep. There was nothing worse than this leaden weight of the eyelids, of trying to focus through the front windows without the helmsman noticing. This morning had not been so bad, because the challenge of the fog, as he steamed south between the South Falls and the Goodwins, was stimulating the adrenalin and forcing him to concentrate.

At thirty-five, Jean-Pierre Le Villain was at the peak of his fishing career. His father had helped him with the loan which had bought the fifteen-year-old *Alouette*, one of the last good wooden boats. Sturdy as the oak from which his boat was built, Jean-Pierre had fished deep-sea all this season; there was nothing left in the Channel and the herring had come down into the North Sea.

He had spent a fortnight off Lowestoft and was anxious to get home to a good market and to the comfort of Yvonne's arms. When the fog had clamped down off the Outer Gabbard, he had succumbed to the temptation to maintain his twelve knots, in spite of zero visibility. These were the days when he was glad he had from the outset invested his capital into good radar and electronics, rather than into an expensive steel hull.

He had been forced to buy the modern radio gear for two reasons: soon the Single Side Band stuff would be compulsory, so why waste money on the old MF which eventually he would not be able to give away? All French ships would soon be compelled to listen on Channel 11 to the CROSSMA reports from Cap Gris Nez. He had resented the loss of liberty, but this morning he could appreciate the reasons; the half-hourly broadcasts had been crammed with warnings to keep clear of the southern Sandettié area. A ferry had sunk after collision with a tanker which was now stranded on the bank. A hovercraft had caught fire and the English were out in their numbers searching for survivors – must be nasty in this fog . . .

Apparently, an English frigate was controlling events, so when Jean-Pierre reached the South Falls, he decided to keep clear and not to hinder the rescue work. He left the buoy close to port at 0212 and set course 130°, knocking *Alouette* down to eight knots. He would cross at right angles, keep well above the Sandettié lightvessel and the tanker, then cross the banks to reach the inshore lane off the Outer Ruytingen. He would lose only an hour and a half on his ETA, in the final reckoning – and if he was to wear his halo today, he might as well do the job properly . . . so, at two-thirty, as the first light of dawn stole behind this wretched fog, he told the bosun to use the watch-on-deck as lookouts. It was comforting to see their shadowy outlines crouched into the corners of each wing.

He peered for the hundredth time into the darkened radar. Echoes were passing slowly down the south-west lane and the north-east route was crowded; there were several anchored ships and he could pick out clearly the large blip of the tanker on the Sandettié bank. Those other small echoes clustered near her must be the tugs . . . *Alouette* would pass three-quarters of a mile north-ward of the tanker, but he would lay off a bit more for the tidal stream which was still setting south-westerly.

'Bring her round to port – steer 115°.'

He noted the time, 0242, in the log, then went outside to the starboard wings for fresh air; with the warmth of the new day, the wind might get up and disperse the fog. There was a chance later in the forenoon, because the *metéo* was forecasting wind from the north-east. Things might improve, once south of Gris Nez. He swept back his black hair, content to feel the freshness of the morning breeze.

'Captain . . .'

Meyrac, his oldest and most reliable seaman, was pointing across the port bow. His head was cocked to one side, as he peered into the lightening dawn. 'Captain,' he repeated, 'I heard something. Sure of it. Cries in the water – *écoutez* . . .'

Le Villain moved to the bridge-side and inclined his head. The diesels throbbed, the sea hissed along the water-line.

'Stop the engines,' he ordered briskly. 'You may be right, Meyrac. We'd better make sure.'

'That's what we used to call "first light", Ella,' Guy Hannen said, trying to control the chatter of his teeth. 'Dawn's coming up.'

He was in the water and clinging to the lifeline of the rubber dinghy. Shivering uncontrollably, he was counting the minutes before he would give up and allow Ella to take his place.

His wrist-watch was still working, and it was some time after eleven last night that she had insisted on slipping over the side to change places with him, whilst he regained his circulation. The constant effort was draining both their strengths and they could not keep this up much longer . . . the flesh of his legs and his hands was numb and had taken on a corpse-like pallor . . . if the old man died, he could slip the body over the side. There would be room for one more in the dinghy.

After *Ypres* had sunk, the raft had been encircled by pathetic groups of survivors in the water. Night had closed in, but they had rescued two women, one a middle-aged Belgian, the other a German girl. He had just shoved them into the bottom of the flooded dinghy, when it brushed against what he thought had been a corpse. Someone had lashed the body to a wooden seat, but an old man's voice had cried out, quavering in the darkness.

Ella and he had slipped the conscious man over the rounded rubber gunwale; he had been lying in the bottom of the dinghy ever since. The women had taken turns in fanning the old man's flickering will to live, but someone had to be over the side, for there was no room for them all . . . and during the terror of that interminable night, the children had remained amazingly calm. Little Lucy had stopped her silent sobbing, as Mark held her head against his chest, trying to keep them both warm.

Guy had succeeded eventually in erecting the orange hood which had helped to keep them warmer as they drifted on the tides. The moaning of the lightship's siren regularly every half-minute had fretted their nerves and made sleep impossible. Then they had been swept down again towards the anchor bell of a ship which seemed to be stopped somewhere between them and the lightship . . . all night long, the fog-horns had brayed their miserable concert and the bells had rung.

Just before midnight, Guy thought he had seen a blaze of light and the roar of engines. He had organized them all to yell together, to blow their whistles – and he was sure he had heard a loud-hailer blaring orders – but it had all been unintelligible and a nightmare of shattered hopes. The raft had been turned by the flood tide and been taken up again towards the north-east. His diminishing hope was that they could hold on until the fog cleared.

He had been in the water, on and off, for nearly seven hours – his mind was beginning to wander and he was losing the urge to struggle. This, he realized dimly, was the onset of exposure, the loss of the will to survive. Too easy to let go – to slip away on the tide before Ella noticed his disappearance. Was that why she was clutching his wrist? As he fought against black despair, her fingers were pinching his sodden flesh.

'Guy, listen . . .'

Above the slap of the wavelets, he heard the slow pounding of diesels, the coughing of exhausts.

'Yell – *all together* . . .'

Their feeble cries grew into a ragged crescendo: the advancing ship was running them down. Hannen tore the whistle from his life-jacket and blew with the last ounce of his strength. He could hear Ella leading the yelling and the whistling – and then the ship throbbed past them, invisible but very close.

The rubber dinghy bobbed in the wake and he knew that the

ship had gone. Ella was stuffing her fist into her mouth to stifle her frustration. She was staring at him, tears streaming down her oil-streaked face; she turned away from them, her shoulders racked by her bitter, silent sobbing.

The rattle of an anchor cable, not far away – the slow coughing of diesels and then a ship's bell ringing . . . French voices in the fog and the squeal of a pulley block.

'Yell your heads off! All together . . .'

There was an answering, unintelligible shout through the mist. He blew on his whistle – listened . . . back came an acknowledging Gallic response.

He heard the 'plop-plop' of an outboard coughing slowly towards them. They continued shouting until the snout of an orange inflatable lunged on top of them.

The French fisherman towed the survivors back to the trawler wallowing in the undulating swell. They hove out the women and children, then gently handled the injured old man up the wet sides. The old fellow was dead by the time they had slipped the bowline beneath Hannen's armpits.

CHAPTER 22

Harbour Master, East Thames

0715, Friday, 4 June
Wind: Force 3/4, ENE
Visibility: Hazy, 1 mile

Captain Stuart Gratton slipped into overdrive and let his Lancia have her head, as he swung out of Rochester and on to the motorway. He was feeling remarkably spruce after such a short night, but he needed this uncluttered road to collect his thoughts before reaching his Harbour Master's office. It was just after seven and he would be in Gravesend before the roads became clogged.

He enjoyed these emergencies: they tested the fine tuning of the organization and high-lighted the occasional weakness, as well as the *esprit*, of the team. A good old panic was a tonic in this humdrum existence. He felt exhilarated, in spite of the tragedy in the Straits; the departmental meeting with the Minister last night seemed aeons ago. He had returned directly afterwards to Gravesend to replan today's movements, after learning of *Bir-Hakeim*'s stranding. He had been the odd-man-out regarding the tugs, but at least Grubb had intimated that East Thames could retain a minimum of two of the powerful tugs among those assigned to the VLCC's swinging manoeuvres this afternoon.

Dermott Tuson had rung at 2330 from St Margaret's Bay. It was thoughtful of him to keep Gravesend in the dismal picture – typical of Dermott. There was no better man around to organize a rescue operation and the St Margaret's Bay Centre would adequately fit the bill. The fog was as thick as ever, so there was

128

little hope for the survivors during the night; it was a miracle there still had been no further incident.

Andrew Brough, Universal's Berthing Superintendent, had come through just after midnight.

'Stuart, the refinery is getting low in crude,' his compelling voice had rasped, '*Bir-Hakeim*'s stranding is bloody serious . . . the improvement in the pound and the holiday allowance has sent the motorists crazy.'

'What can we do for you?'

'We ordered *Niger Petrola* to slow down, north of the Falls, pending a decision from you. London wants to divert her from Fredericia to discharge here. With your help, we could accept her in the terminal on this evening's tide. She's drawing forty-six feet. I realize I'm pushing your team to the limit, but could you pull out all the stops, this once?'

Gratton had hesitated, wary of the oil boys' pressure. He had glanced at the Tide Board.

'Can you have her off the Longsand Head in time to be up at Knock John by 0800 this morning? She'll have the flood under her and could anchor in the Knob by high water. She could take Kilo One billet, so long as the visibility holds. If not, she'll have to stay in the Black Deep anchorage. We would start moving her up on the afternoon flood, all being well.'

'Is it "yes", then?'

'No, Andrew, not yet. We'll have to look at her planned passage first; it should be okay, if I can adjust the other movements.'

'It'll be good to have your Bill up here – haven't seen him for some time.'

'Yes,' Gratton said shortly, 'but you realize, Andrew, that it's only because I've insisted on the two big tugs that it might be possible. The panic off Dover has taken every tug for miles around. After the Minister's appeal, they've been flocking down there like vultures.'

'Thanks, Stuart. We'll bring her in, then: Kilo One at 0800.'

'Don't push me, Andrew. I'll do my best. Ring through her details for clearance as soon as you can.'

Gratton had remained in the operations room until there was no more to be done. Then he had returned to Rochester at 0200 and woken Judy. She was not overjoyed at her awakening but she cheered up when she heard about Bill – she would come up to Gravesend in the evening to welcome her son home.

The Lancia responded to pressure better than Stuart Gratton did. He was not happy about giving way against his better judgement to pressure from the giants, but this request was an exception. He would support it, provided the visibility held at one mile and the wind did not freshen, when *Niger* would need more tugs. He slipped the car down to third gear and took the back road to the Navigation Centre. He noticed the unmistakable outlines of Mercer's two biggest tugs, *Thor* and *Herakles*, disappearing round Lower Hope point. Even *they* were after the pickings, were they?

He ran up the stairs to his office, a suspicion clouding his mind. He flung open the door and almost knocked down the Duty Officer. 'Sorry, Tony . . .'

'Seen this, sir? They've taken our two big tugs.'

The signal was a direct order: no choice; but three smaller, lower-powered tugs were being substituted.

'Thanks. I'll be in my office.' He slammed the door behind him. So they had deprived him of what he had insisted upon for safety – these politicians were all the bloody same. The Straits would be stiff with craft, but most of them sculling about and unemployed . . . he would have his work cut out to shift these VLCCS – *the ashes of today's programme.*

Utopia – what a far-off dream! He had read that paper of his to the Institute in semi-jocular mood – but the developing maritime nations were already enthusiastically adopting those ideas, unlike the opposition of the old traditional die-hards. We would soon be out-voted in the world conferences which might not be a bad thing if this brought order into things. He picked up the old draft of his diatribe:

'*Coast of Utopia – Marine Traffic Act (Regulation)* – a prissy word for compulsion that . . .

1 All vessels passing through the waters of *Utopia* are to conform with the following procedures, for the general safety, good

order and protection of the coastal and offshore environment.
2 All vessels are to guard 500 or 2182 KHZ and the primary
VHF channel in the prescribed manner.
3 All vessels will be routed and their movements controlled
by the *Utopia* Authority.
4 Vessels with dangerous cargoes will be controlled and
monitored to ensure the safety of other vessels and the protection of the environment.
5 The master will remain responsible for the safety of his
vessel. Belief that compliance with the Authority's orders
imperils his vessel will be a defence for disregarding the
regulations.
6 Vessels are to report to the appropriate radio station at each
Way Point. Twenty-four hours' notice of ETA is required when
possible.'
Underneath he had scribbled: 'Nigeria has already adopted this
off-shore principle.'

He threw the paper back on to the side cupboard. None of this
was achievable without basic area communications.

A galaxy of radio equipment was at hand today but, except for
the Distress frequency under the Conventions, masters were not
compelled to communicate at all for the benefit of area traffic.
They still communicated for their own or their owner's interests.
Today's traffic situation cried out for compulsion in the field of
area radio organization.

A maritime satellite could handle 66,000 'immediate-access'
calls at a time and, when the third satellite was established, there
would be world-wide coverage. With communications such as
this, a shipmaster and his owner could carry on immediate voice
telephone conversation whenever they wished.

Ships should be required to listen out more, so that they could
hear what they needed, instead of having to ask. In submarines it
had been like that: the information was pushed out and the boats
had to listen – or else.

Standard information could be pushed out and repeated on
cassettes – height of tide at Margate or Southend, movement

programme, pilotage information ... A master would instinctively switch on to the relevant broadcast frequency for each category of information when approaching a separation zone or a zonal control area ... the hoped-for 'going map' would guide his actions.

Gratton was dreaming again, but all this could be introduced, if only the will was there ... he had better get back to reality and the job. His team would be working flat-out, juggling the new movements to fit in with these last-minute alterations. A big chap was already swinging off the Universal terminal – it was just about high water. At least one VLCC would be out of the way for this evening ... he had better hurry or he would miss the emergency PLA meeting at nine o'clock.

Fortunately, after leaving the PLA conference room, Gratton had had time to simmer down. The drive back had been difficult and he had been forced to concentrate on the traffic.

He had lost his temper and bluntly told them that he objected to having his orders overruled. It had been a lonely fight, because the fracas in the Straits was outside the PLA's limit. He felt sorry for the manager who must be saying to himself, 'What's that difficult chap Gratton kicking up such a fuss about? Doesn't he realize there's an emergency down at Dover?' Stuart had made his point. They had been remarkably patient with him, even after he had insisted that his objections be placed on record. He had emphasized that if the tide did not make as predicted, if the wind freshened, or if the fog shut in again, he would have to consider cancelling the evening's sailing of the VLCC from the terminal, because of swinging risk. These monsters, with their considerable windage, could present problems of manoeuvre in high winds in the tideway. Then *Niger Petrola*'s movements would have to be cancelled, if she was not already totally committed. He had reached his office in a truculent mood.

His team had *Niger*'s passage diagram plotted ready for him, when Brough came on the phone at 1135.

'*Niger* moves at 1400,' Gratton said. 'Weather and my son permitting.'

CHAPTER 23

HMS *Cumbria*

1155, Friday, 4 June
Wind: Force 4, NNE
Visibility: Fog patches, 100 yards to a quarter of a mile

'No sign of the photographer, sir. The pilot's in sick bay.'

The petty officer saluted, his survival overalls rustling as he left the bridge. Lieutenant-Commander Ralph Latimer, Captain of the Fleet Communications frigate, HMS *Cumbria*, turned briskly to his officer of the watch.

'Take her back to our datum position. Pilot, pass a sit. rep. to the coastguard about the helicopter situation.'

Latimer had been on his feet all night. He was beginning to feel irritable, not so much from the frustration of being unable to carry out a thorough search in this fog, but because of the crass irresponsibility of the ships who were ignoring the repeated warnings from Dover and CROSSMA at Cap Gris Nez.

'Fog's lifting, sir.'

He picked up his binoculars and peered through the gap on the horizon that was opening up on *Cumbria*'s starboard bow. He would be able to see better in a few minutes. It would be a relief to identify visually what he had been carrying in his mind for so long – the plot which his Action Information team had been running throughout the night was blurring in his mind after so long a concentration.

At eleven-thirty, Dover had come through to report that the RAF helicopters were standing-by at Manston. Apparently, from the coastguard clifftop there were signs that the fog was dispersing

– as soon as it was safe to do so, the choppers would be on their way. *Cumbria* was to report when the visibility had improved to a mile and when the cloud base had lifted. Then this bright idiot, intent on grabbing a first scoop of the shambles from a hired Sioux helicopter, thought he would jump the gun . . . the drowned cameraman and the lost chopper were the result.

He had kept *Cumbria* slowly under way all night. As it turned out, had he anchored she would never have reached the un-conscious pilot in time. Something, at least, had gone well amidst this confusion. He left his covered bridge and walked out into the pale sunshine, the first he had seen for days.

Cumbria was under helm and swinging back to her datum position, whence he had tried to control events during the night. Here, two cables from the new landfall buoy and stemming the tidal stream as it changed, he had remained as a watchdog. Now, thank the Lord, there was hope . . . the fog was rolling back . . . there was that bloody lightship, the Sandettié, whose siren, remorselessly hooting every half-minute, had got on everyone's nerves. Her red hull was breaking out from the yellow mist as the sun warmed through. Then a corridor opened up to the north-eastward; the fog lifted round to the south and south-west – but towards the White Cliffs the impenetrable curtain remained.

To port, and less than a mile away, the rescuing hovercraft was standing-by the burnt-out remains of the hoverferry, *Watson Watt*. A couple of inflatables were milling about on their out-boards. Miraculously, there had been no loss of life – the crews must have exercised first-class drill, because there had been some nasty moments . . . at one point the sea was on fire and no one could get near. If she had been half a mile nearer to the beached tanker, there could have been a blazing inferno on the surface of the sea, a situation incomparably worse than that of *Torrey Canyon*; then the only way to put out her fires had been to use the Buccaneers of the Fleet Air Arm which Douglas Parker had sent in with such effect. Latimer had served with this remarkable aviator admiral; he would never forget the man's rolling gait and mischievous humour. But his Buccaneers could never be used here, with all this shipping about.

Bir-Hakeim was showing through the mist, her white side and her red anti-fouling streaked black in this glare. She seemed hard up on the bank, judging by the starboard list she had on her. Her stern was down and little freeboard was showing from along a third of the length of her waterline from her fo'c'sle. It would be a miracle if those tugs towed her off on these tides – they would have to wait for springs and by that time all this filth would have streamed from her – 60,000 tons of crude they reckoned, because the survey which her officers carried out at dawn had brought shocking news.

Her side had been ripped along the water-line by the sinking ferry – not a few tanks, as the first coastguard report had suggested, but the entire length of her cargo capacity. Listing the ship at high water to raise her starboard side, so that the rent could be above water, was the only hope. With her engine room flooded, she had lost all power; they were trying to patch up the hole so that they could pump out and, later, fire one boiler. Then the tugs might tow her off.

Latimer counted over twenty tugs, ocean-going, medium and small stuff, poised like vultures for the pickings. They lay down-tide, clear of the black, serpentine stream welling from the womb of the stricken ship. Bubbling to the surface, it oozed slowly outwards in a widening fan of filth. *Cumbria*'s side was black with the slime. He refused to contemplate the catastrophe if the wind freshened as forecast.

Latimer had taken *Cumbria*, during the night, as close as he had dared to the estimated position of *Ypres*'s wreck. His boats' crews had been searching all night, but so far had stumbled upon only seventeen survivors, two of them terribly injured. The doctor had little hope for one of them, and *Cumbria* had requested immediate transfer to Dover of the casualty by launch. Latimer peered again towards the ferry's last-known position, hoping to see some sign – but there was nothing, not even a mast-head. She must have rolled over onto her side, as she went under.

Communications had been atrocious during the initial phase of the emergency. He was still not clear how many passengers had been on board, because the Belgian authorities were themselves uncertain. *Ypres* had been carrying to capacity over a thousand souls and a packed car deck. There must be terrible loss of life, if the boats had not got away – and, so far, no lifeboat had been found.

He could see a host of small craft making for the area, two and a half miles to the north-east of *Cumbria*. One of the three lifeboats was in the van, combing the area for survivors. Like a mother hen amongst them, the Trinity House buoy vessel, one of the *Princess* ships, was poised to lay her encircling string of wreck and warning buoys; the *Texaco Caribbean* disaster was too recent a nightmare to be forgotten.

On *Cumbria*'s port quarter, a couple of miles to the eastward of the MPC buoy, a line of deep-draught ships was strung out, anchored in the deep patch; it was an amazing sight, a mercantile review of VLCCs, bulk-ore carriers, grain carriers, liquid gas, the lot.

They were guarding the coastguard broadcasts and waiting to proceed up the deep-draught channel, sliding past the stricken *Bir-Hakeim*, as soon as it was prudent to move. Close to the eastward of this line, a stream of smaller shipping was trying to catch up lost time in the north-east lane. Their counterparts in the south-west lane were generally obeying instructions and anchoring off the Falls.

Incredibly, during the night, some ships had still resolutely pressed on down the south-west lane, ignoring all the warnings ... these last twelve hours had been an awakening to Ralph Latimer, Lieutenant-Commander, commanding officer of HMS *Cumbria*.

Two hours ago he had signalled through to C-in-C for another frigate to stand guard by the Fairy Bank at the top of the south-west lane; she could act as a physical presence and try to stop the slaughter. If only the coastguard at Dover could have been given the boats and the aircraft it needed to patrol the Straits. The Operations Centre did its best with an aircraft of the Queen's Flight, since the fast launch had been withdrawn. We were toying with the problem, instead of grappling with it.

Latimer glanced again at the barograph. The last eight hours had shown a definite slide and already white horses were galloping across the Goodwins: Force 4 and the wind freshening from the nor'-nor'-east. France was going to catch the first onslaught of the oil, but when the wind eventually veered, the pollution would befoul the coast from Margate to Brighton. God, he thought, if a fraction of the money that this was going to cost had been invested in proper control of the traffic through the Straits, there would be no need for disasters of this magnitude. What a world we're bequeathing to our children.

He turned to the northward where three spraying barges were nosing through the murk. *Three* sprayers . . . how pathetic . . . and he almost wept as he watched the torrent of black filth swirling in a huge circle, as the tide began to turn at slack water . . . Even if there were five hundred of these units, they would be unable to contain the filth . . . and then the fog rolled in again, shutting out the disorganized armada.

'Start the fog signal,' he ordered. 'Set bridge lookouts.'

He walked out to the starboard wing to conceal his feelings. He agreed with the French: Britain and France should take immediate bi-lateral action rigidly to control the Straits. Our two nations were those who suffered the appalling consequences of an accident – and who had to pay the price of irresponsibility and '*laissez-faire*'?

The wind was undoubtedly freshening; the fog might be blown away, but by tonight the Channel coastline of France would be thick with the sludge of black filth.

CHAPTER 24

CROSSMA, Operations Centre, Cap Gris Nez

1600 (Zone Time – 2), Friday, 4 June
Wind: Force 5/6 NNE
Visibility: 1 mile

Marcel Gobin yawned and stretched himself where he stood on the cliff-top of Cap Gris Nez. It was a grey, miserable day, fog still down to the beach, but visibility improving to a mile to seaward.

He had been on duty for the night watch; he had slept through the forenoon until dinner time, when he had attacked the salami, the veal and the cauliflower for which the navy paid, but which the local restaurant provided. Whatever the others said, he reckoned they ate well here but he missed Paulette's home cooking.

They had found a flat in Le Havre where their first-born had arrived, little Gaston whom they had named after his grandfather. Marcel had decided to remain in the port where he had trained for the Merchant Marine. A couple of voyages to the Far East and then he had begun his year's military service. He had decided to volunteer for the extra month, making a total of thirteen, to qualify as *Enseigne*, Second Class, the equivalent of a Sub-Lieutenant in the British Royal Navy. He was already twenty-two, so was impatient to resume his career in the Merchant Marine.

Marcel yawned again – the watch from midnight to eight was the worst of the three. It had been the devil of a night, the busiest he had experienced since joining CROSSMA, Gris Nez: *Centre*

Régional Opérationel de Surveillance et de Sauvetage pour le Secteur de la Manche – an unwieldy name, but a precise one for the Cap Gris Nez team of twenty-five officers and men.

The lighthouse towered behind them, 236 feet above sea level and overlooking the cliff that tumbled gently down to the shore. The hamlet of Cap Gris Nez consisted of a group of modern, identical cottages for the lighthouse crew and two huts for the CROSSMA personnel.

The lighthouse fraternity had been helpful from the inception of the Operation Centre. Not only had they permitted the new VHF Direction Finding antennae to be fixed atop the lighthouse dome, but they had helped financially towards the building of the Centre poised on the cliff edge at the foot of the lighthouse which had been rebuilt of granite in the early fifties.

Marcel screwed up his eyes to stare into the glare of the fog-bound Pas de Calais. It was extraordinary to realize that throughout that impenetrable blanket an armada lay at anchor; and that a stream of ships continued to pour through the lanes, in spite of the continuous warnings pushed out by St Margaret's Bay and CROSSMA, Gris Nez.

The night had been hectic. Captain Georges de Valence had not returned that evening to his Boulogne home, but had remained at the Centre for the night. He was an efficient and fair commanding officer and the lads liked him. He had pioneered the Centre and, as an *Officier d'Administration des Affaires Maritimes,* he was ideally suited to the job. An ex-Merchant Service Officer, he belonged to the *Corps des Officiers d'Administration des Affaires Maritimes*; a civil servant, whose boss was the Minister of Transport, but whose orders were signed also by the Navy.

All hands had been summoned for the night's emergency off the Sandettié. They had guarded all the frequencies they could and, when St Margaret's was flooded by the traffic, CROSSMA, Gris Nez, had been able to help with the tracking of the multitude of small ships milling about in the nil visibility of the night.

When dawn finally broke, conditions were no better, but more dangerous, for, with daylight, the small ships of the search fleet became over-confident. There had been three collisions between fishing boats but, on the credit side, a Boulogne trawler, *Alouette*, had picked up several survivors. CROSSMA, Gris Nez, had been able to help her back to Boulogne, by bringing her close to the French coast and then tracking her westwards.

Marcel watched a small offshore boat, wallowing in the grey sea at his feet fifty-seven metres below. He turned to the eastwards where the coast disappeared in the murk. For as far as he could see, tangled excrescencies on all the vantage points in the green of the countryside hid the monuments to yester-year's folly; paid for and built by his countrymen when they were under German occupation – the pillboxes, blockhouses and gun-emplacements still littered this once beautiful coast.

The huge concrete fortresses encircling Cap Gris Nez would never be destroyed or removed. One of them acted as a museum, cold and rank in its blackening concrete ten metres thick – and there were many Frenchmen who thought as he did that those who had caused these disfigurements should be forced to remove them . . . but it was too late. Better to forget, forgive and tolerate the returning German tourist.

Marcel wondered what descendants of the French naval captain whose memorial stood on its plinth close to the lighthouse must feel. Encircled by the advancing enemy, the gallant officer and his handful of sailors had resisted until the end.

But the Great Healer was administering the balm of indifference with things militaristic; Marcel's generation were realists – the world must learn to tolerate, but not to forget. That was why he, Marcel Gobin, deep inside himself, did not resent his military service. In an unfashionable way, if he had been forced to reveal his feelings, he was proud to be serving his country, the France which had so bitterly struggled to regain her self-respect . . . Less of this, he had better take over his watch.

He pushed open the door of the operations room, a warm, rectangular space, with windows the length of the wall overlooking the sea. Through these, a constant lookout was kept on the coast and on the shipping passing through the Pas de Calais. Access to the lookout tower on the roof, which held a pedestalled pair of powerful binoculars, was by a circular staircase ascending from inside the ops room; on a clear day, England's white cliffs were clearly visible with the naked eye, but today the tower was useless. The ghosts of Napoleon and Hitler still lingered here.

He took over the watch at his post behind the communications operators; the two seamen, who had joined a couple of months after him, were talking to St Margaret's Bay and to a ship off Cap d'Antifer. The radar operator was already tracking and monitoring the rescue ships in the disaster area.

This most modern of displays, one which could be viewed in daylight, had only recently been installed. When the radar had lived up to its claims, the Centre had been granted the funds to instal it – with the orange markings of the separation zones and its clearly delineated lanes, it was a technological masterpiece: tied to the new VHF direction finder, it could fix the position of any ship within range and, in forty-five seconds, could display its course and speed.

By pre-casting a ship's future position and by monitoring several ships simultaneously, a collision situation was immediately recognizable. But however fantastic the gear and however accurate the plot, both present and future, the expensive marvel could be wasted if the Centre could not communicate with the ships. If they were not compelled to guard a radio frequency the whole exercise was futile. When St Margaret's had watched the *Achilles* affair developing, they had tried to warn the ships, but this had proved fruitless because the ships were not guarding the frequencies.

'The meteo's just come in, sir. The forecast's worse than we thought.'

Marcel strolled to the battery of telex machines clattering on the row of tables in front of the windows: Force 6 to 7 by midnight and already NNE. He moved across to the radar and stared at the picture: *Bir-Hakeim* could not be in a worse position. When the ebb started, the oil would stream towards the French coast.

'Get me the Captain on the phone, Pierre. He may want to alert the authorities.'

He would talk to the British frigate *Cumbria*. She could keep them informed of the exact position of '*les nappes*', the dreaded slicks, as the English called the tracks of the oil.

'The Captain left home ten minutes ago, sir. He's on his way.'

'*Merci* . . .'

Marcel liked the informal atmosphere that de Valence had created here. Unlike their friends across the channel, who were mostly ex-Naval and Merchant Service personnel of retirement age, Gris Nez was manned by the young men who were compelled, like the other Europeans in the Common Market, to serve for one year in the forces, unlike the youth across the channel who were not forced to serve their country.

The door opened and the draught blew a paper from Marcel's desk. Captain de Valence had arrived to take command.

Captain Georges de Valence had enjoyed those last few kilometres of the drive from Boulogne. The coastal road wound through the gentle hills towards the highest point on the coastline of the *Département de la Manche*. *La Manche* to the French was the same as that to the British – but, as a nation, the British were instinctively sea-orientated. His own countrymen, after the recent calamities on the Brittany coast, were at last becoming more alive to the consequences of '*laissez-faire*'.

The hideous gun emplacements which reared at him as he rounded the corner always reminded him of the war which had taken his father from him, a POW for four years, and a broken man at the end of it.

Georges de Valence was born in 1940, so that the war made little impact on his childhood memories. He remembered the Leclerc Division riding triumphantly on their tanks down the Champs Elysées, the ecstatic crowds, the tears coursing down his mother's thin cheeks – and as the years rolled by, he had, like most intelligent Frenchmen, slipped too easily into cynicism. France was a well-governed country, but she still searched for a more just society – it was too simple, as a serviceman, to forget the world outside.

He had joined the Administration after his Merchant Service time, and had climbed the promotion ladder as rapidly as was possible – which was why he had landed this CROSSMA job. Under the direct orders of the *Administrateur-en-Chef des Affaires Maritimes*, Jobourg, he carried total responsibility for surveillance and rescue services in the Pas de Calais area. He could use all the local services if he required them – he would consider alerting them if the situation had worsened during this last hour in the Pas de Calais.

He took a pride in his pioneering job – the surveillance was having an effect, if statistics meant anything . . . but, from his side of the Straits, as the British called them, only an average of four ships a day were reporting the weather and their positions. This situation could improve overnight, once communications were compulsory. He had applied energetically for a guard on Channels 16 and 11 to be made obligatory for all French ships; it would take time to become law, but he had hopes.

The Renault swung round the last bend in the lane threading through the hamlet of Cap Gris Nez. In the next few moments he would learn the worst on the *Bir-Hakeim* disaster. He wished he possessed an exclusive Emergency frequency which he could use, as did the British with their Channel Zero that linked all their emergency services: police, fire brigades, the military, helicopters and lifeboats. The need was so obvious; this latest disaster might rouse the public's anger, so that the money could be voted.

His car door slammed behind him, blown shut by the wind. Surprised, he strode to the cliff edge, hoping that the visibility might have improved; the cliff tumbled gently down to the water's edge, a striking contrast to the sheer precipices of St Margaret's Bay – but he could see no further than a kilometre, where an inshore boat was fishing serenely and presumably without much success: the fish stocks were exhausted by over-fishing, and spoiled by the unchecked pollution pouring into the seas from the northern continental rivers.

Greed was at the root of the appalling and rapidly worsening state of affairs – how could the peace-loving and silent majorities halt the ruthless exploiters of the seas, like the Russian and Japanese juggernauts with their factory ships sucking up everything that swam in the bountiful oceans? Greed, too, tolerated the

Rhine's continued debouching of its chemical and industrial filth into the North Sea. Added to this gigantic river's daily discharge were those of the other northern continental rivers – and it needed little imagination to realize that the life in the seas around our coasts – just as in the Mediterranean – could swiftly die. There was a moment when the destructive process of the ecological chain would be irreversible. Without the sea's bounty – a treasure which had to be nurtured, conserved and rationed – the world would starve.

Marcel Gobin was standing in the doorway. 'Captain Tuson is waiting to speak to you, sir. I've got him on the phone.'

De Valence moved swiftly across the ops room.

'Good evening, Captain. De Valence here.'

'Stand-by, Gris Nez. The Inspector won't be a minute.'

Then the precise voice, which de Valence knew so well, chipped in on the air. They had worked together for nearly two years and a bond had developed between them.

'I've just received HMS *Cumbria*'s situation report, *monsieur*. I'm afraid things are worse than we feared. After the loss of *Ypres* and the stranding of *Bir-Hakeim*, so far we've picked up only nineteen survivors. We can't move in this fog.'

'It's a bit better over here, Captain – about a mile. This wind might clear it.'

'Visibility is definitely improving and *Cumbria* has begun tracking *Bir-Hakeim*'s oil slick. It's a major spillage, I'm afraid. There's little hope of getting the tanker off in my opinion. She has a full cargo – if she breaks up, we've got a major disaster on our hands.'

'What's the direction of the slick, Captain?' De Vale ncesensed the inevitability of the reply, but he needed the precise track. Even with the strong tidal streams running off Cap Gris Nez, the oil would probably end up somewhere near Gravelines, on the next flood or two if the wind persisted.

'*Cumbria* reports a track over the ground of 195°, rate one decimal nine knots. The furthest-on position of the slick at 1600, our time, was half-a-mile due north of the south-west Outer

Ruytingen buoy. We're sorry for you about this, Georges . . . but the wind has only got to veer and we'll get what's left.'

De Valence peered through the windows – no sign yet of the black scum.

'Thanks, Captain. I'll prepare for the worst.'

'I'll send over all I can to help, as soon as the fog clears.'

'Thanks . . . We'll need everything you can muster. Perhaps you'll keep me informed, until we can get our ships out there?'

'Certainly – I'll call you every half hour.'

The conversation came to an abrupt end, as de Valence broke off to summon the navy. Once their ships were monitoring the slicks, at least he could know where the oil was likely to strike. He had decided not to use the sprayers – the ecologists at Warren Springs Laboratory had agreed that the modern detergents were harmless, and that failure to spray was more damaging to marine life than using detergents. Their opinion was that it was safe to allow the oil to drift ashore and then physically to cart it away – thousands and thousands of tons of the filthy stuff, black, sticky and foul. The price of the automobile and the oil-fired generating stations was too high.

'Implement a full Emergency, Marcel,' he ordered. 'Tell the *Gendarmerie* and the *Mairies* that I shall be calling on all available resources. Request them to pin-point the whereabouts of the first oil as soon as they can. Ask the Air Force whether it can track the slicks from above the fog.'

Georges de Valence could do no more . . . he would have to bide his time before issuing his final alert as to where the oil would strike first. He left the room and walked to the clifftop. The fog was lifting to the eastward; he could just see Wissant, breaking through the yellow shroud. The oil might touch there first, between the village and Sangatte. Calais would be whipping out its booms, and Boulogne would be starting to worry.

If the wind turned to gale force, the length of the coast from Dunkerque to Fécamp could be fouled – Gravelines, Calais, Boulogne; then the length of the sandy beaches, Le Touquet, Tréport; on, westwards, to Dieppe and Fécamp – all could be smothered by the foul enemy.

Over 50,000 tons of oil perhaps, spread across the beaches of this, his beloved *Manche* . . . the nightmare, which he had suffered so often, had become reality. He shut his eyes, as the gusts from the north buffeted his body. He heard the seabirds on the beach below, calling harshly to each other as they wheeled into the wind.

CHAPTER 25

Harbour Master, East Thames

1735, Friday, 4 June
Wind: Force 5, NE
Visibility: 4 miles, hazy
LW Thames Haven: 1353
HW: 2026

'Thanks, Stuart,' Andrew Brough called down from the oiling jetty as Gratton nipped back into the Harbour Master's launch. 'Good of you to come over on a day like this.'

Stuart held on to the lip of the canopy as his boat surged ahead. 'Wanted to see for myself how things are going,' he shouted back. 'Glad you got your last one away out on time.'

Brough waved from the terminal above and strode off briskly beneath the range of hose handling gear hanging down like pelican beaks. Stuart Gratton turned in the sternsheets to look at the new refinery. He had been amazed at the speed with which Universal had built this vast complex on the Mucking Flats. The fractional distillation units sprouted in disorderly array between the silver storage tanks gliding past him as his launch slipped down-river towards Canvey Island: he wanted to see for himself the density of the inward traffic waiting to come up.

His team in the operations room had already this afternoon brushed with Braydon Fancourt, the impossible and truculent master of the big container ship *Pollux*. He had tried to beat the gun at low water, before Gratton had given his approval at two o'clock to set in motion the afternoon's movements. Fancourt wanted to slip ahead of *Niger Petrola* before the tanker was committed to the channel. The pilot had had his work cut out to restrain the elderly man who was waiting to 'swallow the anchor' next year. The river would be more serene then . . . but Gratton would miss one of the last representatives of the old school. The cantankerous old boy ran his modern container carrier like a battleship and his crew worshipped the ground he trod. What infuriated him was Gratton's insistence on sending a PLA escort launch ahead of the ship, to clear the way as best it could, because of the explosive cargo *Pollux* was carrying in some of her upper-deck boxes. She was bound for forty-five container berth in Tilbury dock.

It was good to snatch some time in the launch. Gratton felt the wind, a sharp edge of it, as the boat dipped into the short seas building up in Sea Reach. The breeze must be Force 5 north-east, and was sweeping across the Leigh Middle.

Bill would have his work cut out in this and it was as well he was not in ballast, with *Niger*'s gigantic freeboard. Then Stuart sighted the great ship's upperworks, gleaming in the afternoon sun, her twin green funnels tucked gracefully into her modern lines. Her black hull squatted low in the water as she ploughed her way up-river. Stuart felt a twinge of pride. He was glad that Judy had prevailed upon Prue to come up too with the children; a pleasant surprise for the tyro tanker captain.

Gratton had made his decision at 1400 to allow the planned movements to take place. With the shortage of tug power, he was taking a calculated risk – but the demand compelled such initiative. All would be well, so long as Bill could be in the swinging ground by 1945. This should allow enough time to turn her against the last of the flood before the tugs nudged her alongside the terminal at 2026 high water. Whether he could arrive on time depended upon whether the tide made as predicted – *Niger Petrola* would be virtually scraping over the shallow patches, even with her carefully planned passage schedule.

Behind *Niger* Gratton could see the angular shape of the large container ship. *Pollux*, with her dark blue funnel, gleaming in her orange paint and piled high with her boxes, stood out like a block of flats amongst the array of smaller ships waiting for the 'off' from his ops room at Gravesend.

Extraordinary how paradoxical was today's traffic: youth, the coming generation of shipmaster represented by his son, leading the way and accepting the enforced direction from the Thames Navigation Service which his father had helped to sire. Then the ageing generation, in the form of Braydon Fancourt, fading reluctantly from the scene, impatient, resentful at his loss of freedom and unable to accept the inevitable as he brought up the rear. Further out and strewn along the horizon were the sprouting deck cranes from hosts of modern ships – Japanese bulk carriers, the Russian grain carrier *Yalta*, Seabees, roll-on container ships and coasters, and mechanized barges from the Rhine and France.

Modern life certainly does not tarry with yesterday, Gratton thought, as he ordered the launch back to Gravesend. Youth was demanding that progress should develop alongside technology. If there was not enough money to introduce the modern techniques of ship traffic control, it was worth inquiring how the present funds were spent. Some £20 million or more was spent annually by ship owners for providing lights and pilotage off the British Isles – the total must be well over £30 million if all the radio and navigation services were also included. What must the total world cost be?

If the globe could organize and pay for its World Meteorological, World Health and International Civil Air organizations (vast information gathering and transmitting agencies), the shipping fraternities could surely do the same? If the cost of the navigational arts were re-appraised and the money was diverted into, say, track holding or beam riding facilities for ships in narrow waters, the world would have gone a long way towards solving its shipping traffic problems. The ultimate decision would come from society, rather than from the conventions of the sea. He sighed and turned to take a last look seaward . . .

Niger had grown larger already . . . but he sensed something odd about her aspect. The vhf began chattering in the cockpit of the launch – that was Bill's pilot on the air.

'This is *Niger Petrola* . . . A dinghy with three youngsters on board capsized under the bow below Sea Reach Two. Had to go full astern – she cut to starboard and we're now up in the Zulu anchorages. Can you send down a rescue boat to take the kids? . . . Over.'

'This is Gravesend. Roger. I'll send the Police boat. She's down that way.'

'Thanks. We might have to anchor under-foot. Have you any spare tugs to help us turn if we have to?'

Gratton caught the anxiety in the pilot's speech: she was only a few cables from the tail of Leigh Spit and the tide was setting her on. She was bound to touch if she anchored with the tide under her, or if she was unable to manoeuvre back into the fairway . . . The Harbour Master's launch hurried back to base, where he raced up the pontoon ramp.

The operations room was tense, but the duty officer had matters in hand. *Niger Petrola* could not afford to lose a minute, if she was to be up there on schedule.

'Is she up to time?'

'No, sir. But she's back in the channel and going ahead again. Daren't increase her speed: lucky this didn't happen above Number Three with no room at all.'

'What's the tide doing?'

'It's cutting a bit, sir. Almost five inches short, right now. Permission to proceed with the other movements, sir? *Pollux* has again asked for clearance to proceed.'

'Is *Niger* okay now? How much is she adrift?'

'Says she's all right – lost forty minutes, sir.'

Stuart Gratton felt an unease he did not often experience. Things were not going well and the most difficult bit was to come. So much for giving way to pressures and for going against his instinct . . . but *Niger* was committed and there was little he could do about her now.

'Let 'em all come,' he said. 'We've a busy night ahead of us.'

CHAPTER 26

ss *Niger Petrola*, VLCC

2004, Friday, 4 June
Wind: Force 5, NNE
Visibility: 4 miles to eastward, $1\frac{1}{2}$ miles to westward
HW Thames Haven: 2026
LW Thames Haven: 1353

The master of *Niger Petrola* stood on the port side of his enclosed bridge, looking through the window towards Gravesend. A thunderstorm was gathering over Tilbury and it was strangely overcast, though not yet sunset. He still could not pick out the Thames Navigation Service's Centre amongst the hotch-potch of riverside wharves and buildings.

In spite of his fourteen years at sea, he had never before been up the Thames. The pilot was a good 'un, and Captain Bill Gratton had complete confidence in him. After the nasty moment with the dinghy off Sea Reach Number Two buoy, the pilot had taken her up smoothly, under the direction of the Gravesend Centre, using Gravesend Radio. Speeding up where necessary, reducing again to prevent her 'squatting', but all the time pressing on as fast as they dared, against lost time.

The tide guages at Shivering Sands, Southend and Tilbury all confirmed that the tide was not making as predicted – nine inches short, so the last stretch had been dodgy. He breathed a sigh of relief as the West Blyth buoy bore slowly towards them – *Niger* was entering the swinging area and from now it was up to the pilot and his boys.

'I'm sorry, Captain, but the two replacement tugs have been

held up – they're still working another ship.' The pilot was trying to contain his frustration as he replaced the VHF telephone. 'We'll have to carry on with the swing, now that we're committed.' He jerked his head towards the port quarter. 'We're thirty-four minutes late – and it takes time turning a ship of your size here. I hate being crowded. Take a look at that lot . . .' He walked out to the starboard wing and passed his orders to the tugs.

Bill Gratton admired the sang-froid that the average pilot maintained. This angular man seemed unconcerned, though he was two tugs adrift – and underpowered with the other three. He had placed one on each bow and one on the starboard quarter – and he was about to turn a quarter-of-a-million ton deep-draught tanker, with only a couple of feet beneath her bottom, almost in her own length. To make things more trying, the wind was blustery and the flood had petered out earlier than predicted. He was talking to the tug on the port quarter, and explaining his intention of starting the swing to starboard, and so shove her bows into the wind as the last of the flood poked her stern round. 'Better have your anchor ready, Captain. We may need it underfoot if she plays up. Her stern should kick to port, when the engine goes astern.'

Bill Gratton nodded. He wished the pilot would get on with it: there was a queue of shipping a mile long building up astern. It was not easy to stop a ship with the tide under her. Even less so to maintain her heading with the wind abaft the beam; the fairway was too narrow to allow the big stuff to swing across the river – the outward traffic was already streaming down from Tilbury and the upper Docks, so there was little room between the two lanes. The sooner *Niger* could be swung across the tide and out of the way, the happier he would be. The pilot sounded four short blasts, followed by another short, then spoke to the forward tugs. The swinging manoeuvre had at last begun. Both the bow tugs worked over to starboard and the after one went wider to help.

The master raised his binoculars: there was the big container ship, an escort launch scurrying ahead of her importantly, and not more than a quarter of a mile astern. She was proceeding up river and was also trying to catch high water. Between her and *Niger*, in the middle of the river, a tow of three Seabee barges was flogging up astern, loaded to capacity with container boxes, three tiers high. Astern again, as far as he could see, a string of ships was inbound, large and modern, medium-sized and innumerable coasters and barges. Gratton also disliked being crowded.

Glancing momentarily astern, Bill Gratton could pick out the radar scanner on the bluff of Cliffe – when the swing was completed his father might come over in his launch . . . they had been unable to speak again after the Straits passage, but Universal's Berthing Superintendent had said over the phone that the Harbour Master personally had been told of *Niger*'s diversion. It was a curious feeling to know that Dad was responsible for this river and was watching *Niger* at this minute.

'She's very slow, Captain,' the pilot was saying. 'She's not wanting to come up. Where're those damn tugs . . . ?' He smiled wryly, shrugged his shoulders and called for maximum power from the bow tugs. The compass repeater was barely moving and *Niger* lay across the river. The pilot hurried to the side and looked down across the water to the hauling-off buoy.

'The ebb is running, Captain – earlier than expected. A touch ahead on the engine, please. Starboard twenty-five.'

Gratton swung the telegraph to slow ahead, then peered through the window to watch for her foremast swinging up into the wind. To the north-west, a rainstorm was sweeping across Tilbury – thunder could be on its way. The light was failing and it would be dark early.

'She's coming up,' the pilot said. He was darting from one side of the bridge to the other . . . he would have to hasten the turn or she would be swept downstream on the first of the ebb. The heading was 355°, when a sudden gust from the north-east swept off the shore. The swing stopped, just as the ship was gathering headway.

The outer bow tug came on the air: she was giving all she could and the other was crossing further out to starboard to help – but the pilot could no longer risk the advance.

'We'll try a kick astern, Captain. Full astern, please. Wheel amidships . . .' and he used his pea whistle to manoeuvre his tugs.

Bill Gratton moved out to the starboard wing to ensure that the diminutive boat was not girded under the quarter . . . these tug skippers had guts and nerve, the way they flung their small craft about. The after tug was listing inwards and shooting towards *Niger*'s stern. The warp tautened, shivered, sending the spray flying, and then she was giving all the power she possessed.

He felt the strain coming on the tanker even from where he stood, high up in the starboard wing. The light was failing rapidly, but he could make out the Seabee barges cracking up across *Niger*'s stern. The bulk of *Pollux* hovered in the background, her flared bows barely a cable-and-a-half away and pointing upstream. Gratton felt uncomfortable at holding up these other ships who needed to make high water as much as he did . . . *Pollux* looked a fine ship: her upper deck was stacked with container boxes and her squat red funnel was nicely faired in to the after end of her bridge.

He could just see her escorting launch, (*Pollux* must be carrying toxic cargo in her upper-deck boxes) drifting and stopped on the tide, as she waited for *Niger* to clear the channel. He saw a sudden flurry at her stern – she was going ahead, trying to bear away from a dark silhouette that had appeared from under *Pollux*'s bows. A dirty old coaster was cutting under the stern of the last of the Seabee barges; she was trying to overtake between *Niger*'s counter and the barge-tow. Bloody fool – *Pollux* would run her down . . . and at that minute the hooter from the container ship blared one short blast. There was a white plume at her fore-foot and she was coming up fast.

CHAPTER 27

MV *Castello de Sierra*, Coaster

2047, Friday, 4 June
Wind: Force 5, NNE
Visibility: 1 mile
HW Thames Haven: 2026
LW Thames Haven: 0132/Saturday, 5 June

Captain Gonzales Zapiola felt as chirpy as a ciccada from the sierra, as he watched the flares at Shell Haven gliding down his starboard side. *Castello de Sierra* had somehow nosed into the Thames estuary without further bother, after her near-miss on the previous evening with that roaring monster near the landfall buoy. At dawn, Zapiola had stumbled upon Tongue Sand Tower and its whistle buoy, his approximate ETA and Notice of Intended Movement having been passed the day before by the Hamburg agent.

On arrival, Zapiola had told his radio man to get through to North Foreland, but the frequency was so jammed that *Castello* had been put on to Warden Radio which handled her movement from then onwards.

Zapiola had groped his way to the East Tongue buoy where, being a good boy, he had correctly reported his position at the Way Point. He had been ordered to continue up the Prince's Channel and to proceed to the Leigh anchorage above Southend to wait, while he applied for clearance and further instructions.

Warden Radio had had their work cut out understanding his English. Details under paragraphs c, e and h had needed constant repetition: 'c – bound for East Kent Scrap Metal Co wharf above

Northfleet; e – no pilot required; h – details of any hazardous or low flash commodities on board . . . NIL.' His fertilizer drums were innocuous as far as he knew; they were inaccessible and scrap metal was presumably not low-flash material.

The visibility had improved during the early forenoon and he had had no difficulty in picking up the anchorage. He had waited all day for his clearance. He had watched the big tankers, container ships and bulk carriers coming up from the Southend and Warp deep-water anchorage shortly after three in the afternoon; he had kicked his heels until at last his clearance had come through at 1615.

He had belted up-river at full speed, keeping out of the main channel. If he could berth at Northfleet on the tide this evening, he could nip up to London and see for himself whether the city lived up to its notorious reputation. The dirtiest city in Europe, the agent had said with his knowing wink . . . 'And if the English haven't the inclination to clean up the porn and the filth around the heart of their capital city, they cannot be surprised if the value of their pound falls. After all, Piccadilly is what the foreigner first sees, it's the first impression . . .' Gonzales was looking forward to tonight, if only he could get up there in time.

He had gone wild with frustration down in Sea Reach where the big tanker had wasted half an hour when a stupid dinghy had capsized ahead of her. The traffic had been held up and Zapiola had been shaken for a moment when he saw a police launch coming towards him. She had swept by and he had breathed again. Later, he heard on the VHF that she was manoeuvring to pick up the three sodden children.

So it had been all the way up the river, with *Niger Petrola* leading the convoy and holding up everyone. Zapiola had soon discovered that the authorities were too busy to worry very much about a coaster: he had managed to slip inside the traffic to gain several places in the queue.

He had not understood the tanker warning lights at Holehaven Point, and he had pressed on without any interference. Canvey Island with its gasworks and tanks; Coryton and the Mobil Oil tanks; and now the giant Shell refinery at Thames Haven was slipping past, the flare-offs flickering red and orange in the failing light. There was a storm building up over Tilbury, but he could make out the shining new refinery that Universal had built at Mucking Creek. Once *Castello* could pass the laden tanker, Zapiola would be well on his way to make her berth before dark.

There was a large container ship ahead of him. She seemed to be stopped and waiting for *Niger Petrola* who was now right across the river. Steaming up the port side of the container ship was a string of three barges towed by a tug. 'Seabees' they were called, especially constructed for the container traffic. How the hell the tugmaster could see with those boxes stacked three high, was beyond Gonzales's comprehension ... If *Castello de Sierra* could slide under the container ship's stern, she could slip between the Seabees by overtaking to starboard. She would pass under the tanker's stern ... Whistling happily, he conned his little coaster to pass close up the big container ship's port side.

He peered up at her vast triangular transom ... *Pollux* of London. *Castello* was overtaking nicely. *Pollux*'s pilot was glaring across at the coaster as she slipped past. Zapiola grinned as he waved impudently. The Englishman shouted incomprehensibly: he did not look as cheerful as Gonzales felt.

The Seabees were right ahead. If *Castello* could maintain her speed, she could easily slip across the stern of the last barge, ease over to starboard, and cross *Pollux*'s stern. Zapiola would then be clear for a straight run up-river, if only that cussed tanker would get the hell out of it.

He dared not come further to port, because *Castello* was already in the centre of the fairway. The small ships who were outward bound were flashing past him in full spate, so he had better stick to his plan and cross over now to starboard.

'Ease her over to starboard, Adolfo ... and *watch it*,' he called from his position from the starboard side of his bridge. He was peering up at the flare of *Pollux*'s bow, its orange paintwork reflecting the flickering light from the refinery flares. Her bulbous snout was beginning to push up its hillock of water before it: she must be going ahead again. He must get well ahead before he came over to starboard any further. He was probably invisible from *Pollux*'s bridge, so he would cross over before the panic started. There were so many sirens and hooters sounding from the tugs and from other traffic that a small coaster who was ignorant of the rules would cause little 'aggro'.

'Bring her back to port a bit . . . steady on that . . .' He was conning her nicely and there was daylight now between *Castello*'s stern and *Pollux*'s stem . . . Another twenty metres . . . The Seabees were very close, the wash of the last barge slatting against *Castello*'s port bow. He still could not see their tug because of the three-tiered boxes, so there was no need to use his hooter. He would slide across quietly, cause no trouble . . .

'Starboard again, Adolfo . . . *well* . . . that's it . . .'

He remained looking aft across his stern, as the coaster began to crab across the bulbous bow so close under his stern. *Castello* was dead ahead, the truck of the huge ship's foremast being just visible above her flare. A considerable bow-wave was gleaming now, so she must be getting a move on. Then *Castello* was across, very fine on *Pollux*'s starboard bow, thirty metres ahead . . . A hooter boomed above them, one short blast.

Zapiola turned aft to watch his course. The Seabees was almost abeam. Then he saw the tanker's stern directly ahead . . . she was making sternway, blocking his progress up-river.

'Stop her,' he yelled to Adolfo. 'Port ten . . . Cut in under the barge's stern.' *Castello* was safe enough. He would follow the Seabees and try to contain his patience.

Astern of him, three short blasts blared across the river. *Pollux* had been impatient with the tanker all the way from the estuary and she was now in trouble.

'Full ahead, Adolfo.'

He grinned as he lit up his last cigar. He would be docked and moored up in less than an hour.

CHAPTER 28

ss *Pollux,*
Container Ship

2047, Friday, 4 June
Wind: Force 5 NNE
Visibility: 1 mile to westward, 3 miles to eastward
HW Thames Haven: 2026
LW Thames Haven: 0132/Saturday, 5 June

'Braydon,' the company doctor had told him during his medical
four months ago, 'you've got to accept that you're not as young
as you were. You're fifty-three, senior master of the company.
You want to enjoy retirement, surely? If you go on the way you
are, allowing pettifogging irritants to work you up into a fury,
you'll suffer a heart attack within the year . . .'

Captain Braydon Fancourt stood in the port wing of his bridge,
gazing aft at the shipping which was stacking up astern of his
beautiful ship, *Pollux.* He had snatched these few moments while
waiting for that tanker to swing off Universal's terminal. *Pollux*
was safe in the pilot's hands whilst she was forced to wait – and
he needed time to calm down after this evening's frustrations.
They called him 'Fireball' in the ship, but they respected him, he
was sure of that; *Pollux* was spotless and ran to time, provided he
was left to get on with things without interference.

Coryton and Mobil tanks had slipped astern; now the pulsing
light from the flares of the refinery were reflecting against the
gloss of his immaculate funnel. That tanker, *Niger Petrola*, had
been holding him up ever since the Warp.

Today had been the biggest balls-up since Bannockburn; inefficiency all the way, from the moment *Pollux* was retarded by an unfortunate change of plan at the Tilbury container terminal. She had been half-way across from Rotterdam and the alteration had forced him to anchor for four hours, so that he had already been late. Fate had been against him all the way; on weighing he had picked up a length of someone else's cable and clearing it had taken the mate and bosun half an hour. When finally he had moved on up river, as fast as the pilot had dared, that bloody tanker had blocked the channel above Number Two Sea Reach, whilst coping with some idiot dinghy. If he did not make Tilbury Entrance Lock by nine o'clock, *Pollux* would be in trouble; not only would she lose number forty-five berth and the cranes, but she would have to turn again and anchor for the night in the busy river off Northfleet.

'Captain, we can move on up again . . . Engine slow ahead, please.'

Captain Fancourt was watching a damn-fool coaster, filthy, flying her tattered and grimy Liberian flag, passing close under his counter – she was gate-crashing the queue which was waiting to shove on up-stream. The skipper, a dago, his guts hanging over his belt, was wearing dark glasses even in this failing light; he leaned across the front of his canvassed bridge, conning the tramp up-river as he puffed at a cigar. The coaster was abeam and coming up fast, overtaking a tow of Seabees fine on *Pollux*'s port bow. The foreigner was waving up at him. Fancourt snorted, turned on his heels and hurried back to his bridge.

'Seen that fool on our port beam, pilot?'

'No, sir; but I think we can move up slowly – the tanker is beginning to swing. She's slow, but we haven't much time in hand, Captain. The tugs are ready for us at the Entrance Lock.'

'Half ahead,' Fancourt ordered. He would ease down again, once *Pollux* had way on, and was clear of the tanker's counter. The pilot had disappeared to the port side and was peering towards the port bow. Fancourt could not catch what he was shouting.

'Say again, pilot . . .'

He moved across to the port side of the wheelhouse. 'What d'you say?'

'She's right under our port bow, Captain. She's on top of the Seabees – she may even be trying to cut across our bows, by the way she's going.'

Fancourt strode outside for a quick look. The coaster was just visible, her upperworks disappearing beneath the flare of *Pollux*'s bow.

'I'll ease off to starboard,' Fancourt said, hurrying back into the wheelhouse. 'Sound one short blast, officer of the watch. Starboard fifteen . . .' There would be just room to slip under the tanker's stern and still not cross the middle line of the fairway. The gyro repeater began ticking across the heading.

'Steady on 268°.' The pilot was talking through his radio to Gravesend, but Fancourt was more interested in that bloody idiot in the coaster.

He glanced again towards the port bow. The Seabees were still drawing ahead, very fine on his bow, but the coaster had disappeared. The loudspeaker on the bulkhead was crackling. The chief officer was calling from the fo'c'sle-head. 'Mate here, sir. This coaster's a bit too close for comfort. She's right ahead and showing no signs of paying off to starboard.'

'Distance?'

'Forty yards, sir, maximum . . .' The pilot was shouting from the port wing. 'Captain, she's right ahead. *Starboard your wheel.*' Fancourt hurried outside towards the pilot, shouting over his shoulder.

'Starboard twenty. Steer fifteen degrees to starboard.'

He peered over the bridge screen – he could just see the truck of the coaster's mast – *dead ahead*. The man was a maniac. *Pollux* would slice her down the fore-and-aft line, if she didn't haul out swiftly. He stuffed his hands aggressively into the pockets of his reefer jacket and stomped back into the wheelhouse. The pilot was pattering behind him.

'I've reported this fool,' the pilot said. 'He's not fit to be . . .'

He never finished the sentence. He was staring to starboard through the window, apparently mesmerized.

Pollux was steadying on her new heading. Dead ahead, the slab side of the tanker was blocking the channel – *and she was gathering sternway* . . . During her swing manoeuvre she must have gone astern and now she was crossing his bow, *from starboard to port* . . . She was less than fifty yards off and growing vaster with each second that passed.

'*Emergency astern*,' Captain Fancourt shouted from his corner at the starboard door. '*Hard a-starboard! Sound three short blasts.*' He grabbed the mike of the intercom: 'Let go the starboard anchor,' he rapped. 'Then clear the fo'c'sle-head.'

The log repeater was showing five and a half knots. *Pollux*'s head was beginning to swing . . . 291° – 295° . . . He rushed to the bridge screen, as a gust from the north-east slammed against it.

The siren boomed above his head. He steadied himself against the steel of the bridge screen, as the black plating of the tanker's side reared remorselessly towards *Pollux*'s pointed stem. He waited, numbed by the inevitability of the impending crash; they would collide for'd of the tanker's bridge . . . and *Pollux*'s toxic and inflammable boxes were stacked for'd, loaded at Rotterdam and separate from the remainder.

The deck was trembling beneath his feet as the turbines built up to full stern-power. He gripped the rail of the bridge dodger with both hands. There was nothing he could do, nothing but watch his fifty-thousand-ton ship smash into the side of a fully laden tanker.

CHAPTER 29

Harbour Master, East Thames

2030, Friday, 4 June
Wind: Force 5 NNE
Visibility: 1 mile to westward, 3 miles to eastward
HW Thames Haven: 2026
LW Thames Haven: 0132/Saturday, 5 June

'There she is, children,' Grandpa was saying. 'There's Daddy's ship – across the marshes, to the right of those old huts. See her, Prue? She's starting her swing.'

Prudence Gratton smiled as she took over the children from him. He was as excited as a schoolboy, this grizzled man who was her father-in-law. He stood above them, a shaft of tenderness momentarily touching his chiselled face. He crouched down again, angular and ungainly, as he pointed out the sleek ship nosing off the point.

'So long – I've got work to do. Must see that Daddy doesn't hit anything.' They had laughed as he kissed them. Then he turned towards Gran. 'You do the driving, dear. You know the road back to Gravesend.' They had watched him striding off down the Alpha jetty, lean and athletic still. He waved and they watched him in the sternsheets of his launch as she forged out into the stream.

They shared the children between them, she and Gran. The wind was fresh and Prue was glad of the scarf that Bill had given her on their honeymoon. She had tied it around her hair, gypsy-wise. He had little time for sophistication and this was a marvellous, unheralded reunion . . . Bill still did not know that they were here to welcome him. As soon as *Niger Petrola* was berthed, Grandpa was coming back to take them across to the terminal jetty.

'Will we be able to go over the boat, Mummy?' Anthony asked, his saucer eyes staring up from Gran's side.

Prue was holding Emma, still not yet three, in her arms. 'Daddy, Daddy . . . see, Daddy.' She was flapping her hands towards the water.

'Let me take her, dear,' Gran said. 'She's heavy for you.' They stood there, the four of them, three generations, watching the next head of the Grattons bringing his ship up London River.

A serenity had enveloped Prue. It was wonderful to witness the silent pride that the parents felt for their son. True, he was their only son, but they had not spoiled him. During the precious moments in Bills arms, he had once reminisced of his youth and how he regretted having given his parents such a worrying time. Wild and unpredictable, the despair of his housemaster, he had one day made up his mind to go to sea. With a purpose to work for, his attitude had changed dramatically. He had reached his present rank through ability, hard work and the quality of an independent mind. He had never bothered too much about others' opinions; this strength, though a hindrance when young, had stood him above the others as he climbed the ladder of his career – she was sure of that.

'What's that noise, Mummy?' Anthony was cocking his head to listen to the distant ship's hooter – she counted four toots, followed by another floating down on the wind.

'Daddy's telling the other ships behind him that she's turning, I think. Look, the tugs are pulling her round.'

The great ship, her sleek black hull low in the water, looked as though she was taking up the whole river as she began to swing across the tide. A string of small ships was slipping downstream, and keeping close to Lower Hope Point and Blyth Sand. It was peaceful here, in the failing light of evening and the wind. She watched a flight of widgeon flickering high overhead, the gulls below them wheeling and calling in the wind. A curlew was mewing plaintively behind her while a flight of oyster-catchers winged low across the river wall, cheeping to each other; they turned and settled on the foreshore where they scrabbled busily along the line of shingle still remaining at high water. Soon she would have Bill to herself for a few hours, if he could snatch a night off. She sighed happily, astonished at the way the Good Lord had blessed her day.

She watched the rain sweeping across Tilbury shore and all at once the evening became strangely sombre. *Niger Petrola* stood gaunt and stark against the eastern light as she struggled to turn. Innumerable ships waited below her, a brood of pullets impatient for their roosts. A large one, her orange hull prominent amongst the others, a stack of container boxes piled high along her decks, seemed to be drifting very close to Bill – and just ahead of her was a string of barges towed by a fussy tug. There was something, (she could not see clearly in this light) passing between them and the container ship.

The sound of a ship's siren, one short toot, drifted down on the wind.

The Harbour Master had not invited any of his officers to accompany him in the launch this evening. He had wished to be on his own, to savour for once the pleasure which Bill's arrival was bringing to Judy and himself. It would have been a perfect occasion, if it had not been for the hectic day and for the congestion in the Sea Reaches; there were too many small ships taking the law into their own hands – he interrupted a heated protest being passed at this moment by Braydon Fancourt's pilot to Gravesend Operations Centre (he sounded like Captain Alexander, a patient man if ever there was one – and tactfully selected to cope with Braydon, no doubt). A Liberian coaster was giving trouble.

He did not often have the time to enjoy this mysterious moment of a summer's evening, when the Thames languidly settled down for the night. He was normally on his way home or frantically trying to sign the day's correspondence, but there were still moments in his life when he was touched by the romance of this river, the artery of the British people – 'liquid history' as it had once been called.

He half-closed his eyes and gazed into the murk that had descended to the westward – he could almost see the long ships of the Saxons pulling up the river, sails brailed, their burnished shields flashing in the setting sun, oars flicking in the water; then Drake and his men, manning the side of the diminutive *Golden Hind*, as she glided up on the tide to meet their sovereign waiting to honour them at Greenwich; the bitter weeks of the Mutiny at the Nore in 1797 when the country held its breath, its prime defence, its fighting ships, refusing to go to sea – and, so soon afterwards, the shame of the appearance of uninvited Dutch men-o'-war sailing up the river, among whom was one of his maternal ancestors; the bells of London pealing the tidings of Trafalgar; and the city, aflame to the water's edge, when Hitler's bombers came.

Old Father Thames would roll on down to the sea until *homo sapiens* put an end to things through his own stupidity . . . and yet, there was hope. Man's destiny, he was certain, was created to advance, not retard . . . good did, in the end, triumph. Progress *could* benefit the modern world, as well as destroy . . . and, however slow the advance, there *was* a move forwards in his world of ships.

There was always resistance to change; tradition versus new ideas. Thank God for the new generation of shipmasters represented by men like his son. Bill was an ardent advocate for traffic control in the congested areas throughout the world. 'It's too damn dangerous without,' he had said. 'Your propositions make sense, Dad – and the maritime nations will accept them in the end. Before it's too late, I hope.'

A couple of diminutive figures were moving about the port side of *Niger*'s bridge. One of them, short and stocky and smaller than the other, must be Bill. The tanker was having difficulty with her swing and the wash at the tugs' sterns was frothing white in the gloom. The wind was gusting and this must have checked her swing. The bow tugs had slackened off and the after boat was giving all she could. He swore softly to himself – if only they had listened to him and let him keep the two powerful tugs instead of allowing them down to Dover . . . *Niger* was holding up the whole river. The air would be blue on Braydon's bridge at the minute.

The Japanese job and the Russian grain carrier were just appearing, head and shoulders above the rest, and all of them bunching on the slack of high water. There were innumerable small ships slipping up the sides, inward and outward: impossible to control them as well as things stood. All usually went well (ninety-nine per cent of skippers and masters were thoroughly responsible) until a bloody fool, such as that Liberian coaster, insisted on taking the law into her hands. He could see her now, coming up fast abreast *Pollux*'s port side.

What the devil was she up to? He stretched across for his R/T microphone, about to speak to his duty officer at the Centre. A tow of Seabees was close ahead of the coaster, and – *for God's sake* – she was cutting in under *Pollux*'s bow. She was squeezing ahead, between the last of the piled-high barges and the container ship's prow.

'Gravesend, this is Harbour Master,' he began to transmit. 'Log the name of that coaster hazarding *Pollux* . . .' but then his command was annihilated by the boom of *Pollux*'s siren downwind. She was easing over to starboard, to give that fool room – Braydon probably could not even see the coaster.

Stuart Gratton stood up in the stern-sheets, steadying himself against the canopy, as he ordered the launch to turn up towards the Seabees. He felt the wind in his face, as he recognized the figures of Fancourt and his pilot leaning over their port wing. There was a convulsion in the black water at *Pollux*'s stern as she went ahead and began to turn away to starboard.

Collision was imminent. This was that second which no ship's captain forgets, if ever involved in collision. This was the unforgettable, when no more could be done to avoid calamity. He held his breath; powerless, an ineffective observer, waiting for the agonizing crash of impact.

Niger Petrola was making sternway, back into the river, her stern tug broad on her port quarter and pulling like fury. The Seabees had passed clear and were up-river of the tanker's transom. Close under the tow's last barge, the bows of the coaster were appearing again as she tried to regain the middle-line of the river. Then he heard three short blasts as *Pollux* went full astern.

The huge container ship had considerable way on her – she seemed to be under full starboard rudder. The two men on the bridge had disappeared to the other side – and *Niger*'s transom was rearing out of the murk, thrusting into the stream.

The distance between the two leviathans steadily decreased. Half a cable, then fifty yards, the dark gap between them closing like sliding doors. As the wedge vanished, the first abominable screeching of rending steel shattered the peace of the evening.

Gratton could not tear away his eyes. The sharply-angled stem, prominent in its orange paint, slid across the black plating of its adversary. The forefoot bit deep into the vitals of the laden tanker, forward of Bill's bridge. The din of the buckling steel seemed to continue interminably – and then the container ship could advance no further.

An uncanny silence followed. He was aware only of the coughing of the exhausts of the launch as the coxswain put her astern. He heard the mewing of the seabirds, the clatter of a goods train shunting in a railway siding. Then, while he held his breath, praying that the worst was over, a blinding light flashed from forward on *Pollux*'s upper deck. A flame flickered, then burst into an orange glow; a nucleus of crimson and green glowed slowly along the deck level. There was a blinding sheet of flame . . . then pin-points of fire were dancing on the surface of the jet black water.

Epilogue

0210, Saturday morning, 5 June
Wind: Force 6/7, NNE
Visibility: 5 cables, obscured by smoke

The Harbour Master sat alone in his office, listening to the murmur of orders emanating from the ops room. This was the first moment since the disaster when he had been able to snatch a moment's rest: ten minutes past two – over five hours since the moment of impact. He was numbed by the shock and reaction had not yet set in.

The impossible had happened. Fate had ordained a chain of blunders to coincide in one horrendous moment. He and his old Chief had talked of this twenty years ago – their whole endeavour had been to make impossible such a calamity. Now two big ships had collided in the Thames. The tanker had exploded because of the low-flash cargo in the boxes on deck in the fore-part of the container ship. Stuart had set in train from his launch the executive order for POLOCAP, the emergency procedure they had worked out with such care and which had been exercised so often.

The Duty Officer had used his initiative and despatched Judy and the family back to Rochester. Stuart hesitated yet to phone the appalling news; he could not yet absorb it himself. He shut his eyes to blank out the horror, but a flickering red mist danced beneath his lids from the crimson glow of the river which was still afire.

The firefloats had eventually arrived on the scene, delayed because of the confusion over who was to take priority of the remaining tugs. Not only was it Friday night, when everyone had taken off for the weekend, but the river had been denuded of the powerful fire tugs with their high capacity pumps.

The auxiliary craft could not yet approach close enough to the burning tanker, but Bill, before they had taken him off in the ambulance, had managed to save the survivors of his crew. His ship was still a raging inferno and her oil was still pouring from her ruptured tanks and adding to the sea of fire drifting down on the ebb. If the fire-fighters had not succeeded in extinguishing the flames before low water, the blazing surface could drift upstream, when the flood began running again.

Thank God *Pollux* had managed to drag herself clear. Fancourt, with that dash of decision which made him a fine seaman, had proceeded at full speed up-river out of the holocaust, the bows of his ship crumpled back as far as his foremast.

The threat of floating crude had forced some of the power stations to shut down, afraid for their cooling water and condensers. There was a partial blackout in the area and the hospitals were hard pushed to cope with the casualties that had been trapped in the disaster. The trains, except for the diesels, were at a standstill and the police had a job to clear the roads for essential traffic.

This night was worse than any Stuart Gratton could remember since the blitz; more agonizing because of the appalling consequences. Thousands of tons of oil were pouring filth along the marshes and into the creeks. There would be no end to this – the after-effects would last his lifetime.

He rose to his feet in despair. He buried his face in his blackened hands and wept. No one could see him here, could witness the agony that was killing him. He flung open the window. The acrid stench of fire and oil burnt his nostrils. He cried out savagely to his God to save his son lying unconscious, terribly burned, in the emergency ward. Prue was on her way to the hospital to be by his side. He would try to get through to Judy. He picked up the phone as the tooting of a tug sounded distantly down the river. And a sea-bird called, lonely, from the marshes.

APPENDIX

What of the Future?

'If this is the point we have now reached, what of the future? Most people will agree the time has come to emphasize the need for an "area mentality", from which the affairs of traffic flow can be governed. We need to think larger than we do at present, when organizing what we kid ourselves are traffic systems, but which, in reality, are collections of loose ideas.

'Shipping is international and implies commerce. And commerce implies development. We cannot avoid change any more than we can refuse choice. The vital catalyst must be communications, without which neither trade nor transport can flourish, nor the safety of movement or the environment be assured. The rational use of these communications, in their fullest sense, must therefore be allowed to supersede the conventional, in the furnishings of these coastal highways with their contribution to order and conformity.

'Then there will be – at least – the basis for an International Convention for Sea Traffic to ensure standards and uniformity of conduct, as the airways enjoy. But, until then, we will continue in Alice's Wonderland.'

October 1976   *Lieutenant-Commander R. B. Richardson*